THE SEA HORSES

JENNY HUGHES

THE SEA HORSES

ISBN: 978-1-934983-11-9

Stabenfeldt, Inc.
225 Park Avenue South
New York, NY 10003
www.pony4kids.com

Available exclusively through PONY.

CHAPTER ONE

I didn't like where we lived. We've moved around a lot, Mom and I, but this town was easily the worst. It's big and ugly with concrete buildings and hardly any trees or grass. My school was big too and I spent half my day wandering along endless corridors trying to find whichever room I should be in. I could have asked, of course, should have made friends so I could just tag along with them, but I'm pretty shy and find stuff like that difficult. It seems like everyone was settled in his or her own groups, and although some of them smiled and said hi to the new girl, no one bothered much with me.

I'd had a few months of this, so you can understand why I couldn't wait to get home, dump my books and my school clothes, pull on some jeans and head off to meet Jade.

Jade was, and is, totally my Best Friend Forever. She's beautiful, talented, clever and sweet – everything you'd find pretty sickening in a B F F – except that Jade is my very own darling pony! Mom made the decision to buy a horse for me when I was ten and she and my dad split up.

"I'm going to be the breadwinner from now on, Caitlin," she'd said, giving me one of her bear hugs. "And you know what that means. I have to be where the work is so you'll have to put up with moving from town to town. Jade will be your constant; wherever you go, she goes too."

That was nearly five years ago and I'd grown to love the gorgeous bay pony more and more every single day. She had the temperament of a saint, taking each upheaval happily in her stride, settling immediately in the new field or stable we found her and, unlike me, enjoying herself and making friends with her new companions. I'd felt so guilty when I unloaded her from the truck and showed her where she was going to live this time. Bexworth Riding Center is on the edge of the sprawling town and is well run with big, airy loose boxes for the horses and a fully equipped indoor ring, but it has hardly any land for grazing. The ponies are put into a field on a rotation, each having just a few hours a day and, knowing how much Jade loved being outdoors, I absolutely hated the restriction. She, being Jade, was very good tempered about the hours in her box and I spent as much time as I could keeping her company. It was getting near the end of the school year and I was looking forward to summer vacation when we'd be together practically all day, every day.

"Only two weeks to go," I said, pulling her velvet ears gently as she leaned against me. "Mom says we can go out into the country, and ride anywhere we like. We'll take a picnic and you can eat all the grass you want."

She blew down her nose thoughtfully and nudged me agreeably.

"Maybe we'll spend a week somewhere – no, it'll only be a few days because she has to work," I babbled on to her as I always do, "but we'll have a good vacation, I promise you."

As usual I spent longer than I meant chatting and grooming, and by the time we'd done forty-five minutes in the ring, followed by another lengthy session in her stable, I was late getting home.

"Caitlin, are you OK?" Mom sounded worried.

"Yeah, fine. Sorry, did you wait to eat?" I hurried into the kitchen.

"No," she said, all flushed and excited-looking. "I thought we'd go out tonight, sort of a celebration. How's Jade?"

"Great. We did some flat work and tried a couple of jumps."

"Sounds good," she said, bustling around tidying up, something that doesn't come naturally to her.

"It was all right, but we'd both rather be galloping across a meadow or somewhere."

"Of course you would," she said and stopped trying to force a cereal packet into an already full cupboard. "And – well maybe you'll be doing that sooner than you think."

"OK," I sighed. "Tell me what's happening. You're changing jobs and we're moving again – right?"

"Well, um, not right away because so far this is just a one-time thing, and if I mess up they won't want me again."

"You won't mess up," I said.

She's a fantastic photographer, specializing, or at least hoping to specialize, in pictures of wildlife.

"Thanks, sweetie, but this could be the big one!" She named a high profile publication. "They're paying for me to spend a couple of weeks or so on the Galapagos Islands and if they like the results –"

"Wow!" I knew what this meant to her. "You've always wanted to go there!"

"I promised myself I'd go once you were grown up," she said and bit her lip. "But this is just too good an opportunity to pass up, so –"

"So?" I looked at her curiously. "What's the problem? Because there obviously is one."

"Well, for a start, it's the longest I've ever been away."

"No it's not. That bird watching gig took nearly a month. Four weeks of getting up earlier than usual for once."

"Ooh, sassy," she still wouldn't meet my eyes.

"Oh no!" The realization hit me. "You mean you're going without me! You're going to leave Jade and me stuck here in Bexworth!"

"No, of course I'm not," she said, rubbing a hand violently through her hair.

"Don't do that. You look like a middle-aged punk rocker," I said. I couldn't believe she was going to abandon us.

Most of her work is done from a city office, or wherever it happens to be at the time, and she flies or drives to a location, returning to the office where she develops and edits her photos. Sometimes when a "special," like the bird watching assignment, comes up, the three of us take off together and rent a vacation cottage or something, but she's never ever taken on a project that takes her away on her own.

"Caitlin, honestly this is something major!" her hair was still sticking up in spikes. "If I get this right it means a long term contract. We could settle somewhere really nice instead of moving from one crummy town to another."

"Somewhere nice?" I reached out and smoothed her hair. "Somewhere with land for Jade? Somewhere with real riding?"

"Absolutely," she said fervently. "The company is

international. I could work from home and do everything through the Internet instead of having to check into an office every day."

"Yeah, well it sounds great, and of course you've got to give it your best shot, but –" I paused. It felt selfish to be saying, "but what about me?"

"I know," she said, moving in for a hug. "You can't be left here, obviously, so I found some websites and thought you could choose before we go out tonight."

"Choose?"

"A vacation. I don't have to leave till school's finished, so you can spend the time I'm away having a great vacation."

"On my own? I get to stay in a hotel or something on my own. Terrific," I did a double take. "And what about Jade? There's no way I'm leaving her –"

"Of course you're not," she interrupted, dragging me off to her little study. "Where you go, she goes, I know that. So take a look at these websites, all riding vacations where you take your own horse. There are centers up in the mountains, along river banks, the coast – or, hey look, there's a place that's right in the middle of the wild countryside!"

I sat down in front of the computer and started scrolling. The country one was great, and there was a place in a lush green valley where the riding looked terrific, but to me one place stood out.

"Beacon Lodge," I read aloud. "Acres of grazing, schooling facilities, cliff top rides, beach picnics and a varied competition program."

"Sounds good," Mom said. "But then they all do. What's special about that one?"

I pointed to a picture on the Beacon Lodge home page where a group of young riders was cantering through the spray on the edge of the ocean, while further out, two horses were swimming blissfully with their smiling owners.

"I've always wanted to swim in the sea with Jade," I closed my eyes at the thought. "She'd love it."

"Yeah? That's the one then. And you'll be doing competitions too. You said you wanted to enter more horse shows."

"Yeah, I do," I was still transfixed by the photograph of the swimming horses, noticing the way the light glinted on their sleek, wet skin and turned the waves around them to silver.

"That *does* look great," Mom looked over my shoulder. "So if I get you and Jade booked in there you'll forgive me?"

"Don't be silly," I turned and grinned at her. "There's nothing to forgive."

"That's my girl. Come on, let's go out and grab a pizza."

I dived in the shower to remove any traces of horsiness. I always think smelling of Jade is a good thing, but not everyone agrees. The pizza place was buzzing and I felt a matching stir of excitement at the prospect of the vacation. I couldn't wait to tell my pony, of course, and left even earlier than usual to make my early morning call at the stables. The yard was deserted, very clean and tidy, and only a few horsey heads were looking out over their doors, blinking at the first pale rays of the sun. I walked quickly to Jade's box and looked in. She was still asleep, stretched out on a nice deep bed of hay, her breathing slow and rhythmic. As I slid back the bolt and stepped inside she woke, lifting her head to look at me.

"Hello baby," I crooned. "I've got some news!"

She made her usual welcoming sound, gently blowing through her nose and nudging me happily as I curved my arms around her neck. When I first got her she'd always get to her feet immediately when I approached if she'd been lying down, and it took months before she trusted me enough to let me sit alongside her. Now, though, she just loved to lie with me while I cuddled and petted her, nestling against me more like a cute puppy than a 14.2 hands high, well-muscled pony. I told her all about Mom's job opportunity, and of course about the fabulous looking Beacon Lodge.

"Acres of fields, you can live outdoors all the time – and the riding! Jade, it's going to be fantastic. We can improve our jumping, maybe try cross country and guess what?"

She pushed her nose firmly into me as if to say, "Go on, tell me."

"It's right by the beach! We can go swimming in the ocean together!"

Yeah, all right, maybe Jade didn't understand all the words but she could tell from the tone of my voice that I was excited and happy so, being my Best Friend Forever, she felt the same way too. I got her ready for her morning exercise, another forty-five minutes in the ring and although she put in a good session, she ended it with a series of exuberant little bucks that nearly sent me over her head.

"A few good gallops along the cliff top will soon settle your nonsense," I said, kissing her nose as I removed her bridle. "You've got too much excess energy, Jade. Wait till we can burn some of it up on this vacation of ours."

I was looking forward to the experience so much that the last two weeks of school really dragged. I knew we'd been lucky to get a spot at Beacon Lodge. Mom had managed to grab a last minute cancellation and was busy making arrangements for a trailer to take my pony and me on the journey to the coast.

"I just hope you're going to enjoy this as much as you think," she said, watching me indulgently as I bounced around my room working out what to pack. "And you don't seem at all bothered about missing me. I'm officially offended, Caitlin."

I stopped prancing around with a T-shirt on my head and gave her a quick hug. "It'll be weird not having you around, but you'll be having a wonderful time too, and I've got Jade, remember."

"It would be nice if you managed to make some human friends too," she said, rummaging in my hamper. "Any chance, you think?"

"Yeah maybe," I said cautiously. "We're bound to have a lot in common, aren't we? You know, all being riders and horse-lovers together."

"Mm, though I've never seen anyone quite as besotted with their pony as you are," Mom said darkly. "You don't even bother with boys! I'll put this sweater in the machine. It's your favorite."

"Thanks," I said, grinning at her. "Don't tell me you're trying to get me hooked up with someone! I can't stand the guys at school; they're a bunch of morons."

"Charmingly put. Maybe you should consider what you say before sharing that kind of opinion with your fellow guests at Beacon Lodge."

ry. How many others will there be? Did they tell you you got the booking?"

"They take six and this time it's evenly matched, three guys, three girls."

"Oh, I'll see if I can get married to one then," I said mockingly. "Only Jade will have to be bridesmaid of course."

She responded by tipping the rest of the hamper over me, and we spent a spirited ten minutes having a sock fight.

"I don't know about your horse," she panted as I pelted her with the hated school gear, "but you could use some energy expending of your own – I just hope swimming in that ocean is going to calm you down too!"

❀ ❀ ❀ ❀ ❀

At last, though it felt like months rather than weeks, the great day arrived. Jade and I were leaving at 8 o'clock in the morning and I was up and ready to go before Mom even surfaced.

"Come on, lazy," I thumped on her bedroom door. "I know your flight's not till this afternoon but you've got to see me and Jade off soon."

She stumbled into the kitchen with bleary eyes and tousled hair and squeaked when she saw the time.

"It's practically the middle of the night! You aren't leaving for three hours!"

"I have to give Jade her breakfast and get her and her stuff ready for the trailer," I said, defending myself. "And you're taking my backpack with all my clothes and stuff, remember, so you've got to come with me."

"You go to the yard now and manicure your horse's hooves or whatever," she grumbled, turning back to her room. "I'll join you at eight to say goodbye."

14

"You've got to say it properly," I yelled at her retreating back.

"OK," she yawned. "Seven thirty then."

Honestly, I thought. How she's going to make it if they want her to photograph something at dawn I just don't know!

I made my usual fuss over Jade, but instead of riding her I gave her an hour in Bexworth's small paddock while I mucked out her stable and got all her tack and everything ready to take with us. She enjoyed stretching her legs in the field but trotted over to the gate immediately when I whistled for her. By the time the trailer pulled into the yard I'd done everything and was glad to see Mom's little car following the truck in. She rushed over with my backpack and some sweets for Jade and me on the journey, and for one awful moment I thought she was going to cry.

"So – you're all packed too, I hope," I made my voice brisk and happy. "Passport, tickets – oh and don't forget your camera!"

"I think I've got everything," her lower lip was still trembling a bit. "But it still feels unnatural to be going without you."

"It'll be great," I said firmly. "Think of all those exotic creatures you're going to capture on film. Best photos ever seen, remember."

"I'll do my best," she managed a bright smile and a hug. "Make sure you and Jade have a good time."

"*No* problem," I clambered into the truck's cab and waved cheerfully. "Bye, Mom."

As we drove out of the yard I could see her in the rear view mirror, still smiling bravely, and I waved till she was out of sight, then kept my head turned resolutely to the window so the driver wouldn't see the big, fat tear that was trickling down my face. He didn't mention it, not being so much tactful as taciturn. We drove the long miles to the coast without saying very much at all and I found the breezy confidence I'd shown ebbing slowly but surely away. What if Beacon Lodge was nowhere near as good as it claimed? What if the paddocks were horrible, the surrounding countryside ugly, the sea too rough to swim in? What if, I thought with rising panic, the people were nasty and instead of the smiling, happy faces of the riders I'd seen in the photo, they were a miserable, bad tempered bunch? What if –

"There it is," the driver spoke at last as he pointed ahead. "Beacon Lodge."

A long driveway wound its way between neatly fenced fields of lush green grass. There were trees and flowers everywhere and in the distance, a beautiful old house glowed in the early afternoon sun. A lone rider mounted on a fine black Thoroughbred was waiting at the gate as we slowed down to make our approach.

"Hi," he said, leaning forward and smiling at me. "You must be Caitlin. I'm Zak Meadows, son of the owners. Welcome to Beacon Lodge."

CHAPTER TWO

Whenever I see someone riding I always, always look at the horse before I check out the rider. This one was a real stunner, the color of gleaming ebony with the fine head and classic lines of a Thoroughbred. I noted the strong curve of his neck and his kind, dark eyes and knew from his superb muscle tone that in motion he'd really be something to see.

"Hello," I greeted his rider almost absently. "Yes, I'm Caitlin."

"Great," he sat back and I looked at him properly for the first time.

He was nineteen or twenty, I guessed, tall and slim but well muscled and he had the brightest blue eyes in the most handsome tanned face I'd ever seen.

"I'm just taking Jet out on a – sort of errand but we won't be long," his smile was nice too. "Drive straight into the yard and there'll be someone there to welcome you."

"Fine, thanks," I watched him turn Jet and move away, trotting on the springy grass trail before flowing effortlessly into a canter.

"Down here?" The monosyllabic driver put the truck into first gear.

"I guess so." I looked out of the window with interest and was about to jump down and open a big double gate when it swung open easily and we drove, finally, into the Beacon Lodge yard. It was beautiful; not too big, with a dozen or so stables clustered companionably around the paved center. A tall man, middle-aged and balding, but with features startlingly like Zak's, walked toward the truck, a big smile on his face. I hopped out of the cab and held my hand out awkwardly. He shook it politely and we swapped names – his was Ed Meadows – then he asked if we'd had a good trip.

"Fine thanks, but can I get Jade out right away?"

"Of course," he said. He and the driver unhooked the ramp and I led my beautiful pony down it, stroking her neck proudly.

"Very nice, Caitlin," Ed's voice was approving. "And not a drop of sweat on her either."

"She's a really good traveler," I said, still checking every inch of her, though, while Ed unloaded all our stuff from the truck.

He offered the driver a drink but Mr. Silent shook his head and said he was going to park somewhere and have a nap in the cab before he set off back to Bexworth.

"Hiyah! Ooh, I like your horse." A girl about my own age, with short dark hair, came moving quickly toward us, also beaming.

"Thanks. She's Jade and my name's Caitlin. Do you – um – work here too?"

"No I'm Millie, a guest like you, but this is my second time at Beacon Lodge so I'll show you around if you like."

Ed grinned at her. "Hey, I thought that was my job!"

"Oh, you're busy and Caitlin would rather get the low down from someone like me."

18

He picked up my saddle and grooming kit and raised his eyebrows at me. "Let me stow this stuff in the tack room and I'll be right with you."

"It's fine with me if Millie wants to do it," I said diffidently, feeling shy at the unaccustomed attention. "The main thing I want is to get Jade settled, and I'll probably take a long time doing that."

"You're the last one to arrive and everyone else has chosen to turn their horses out, but you can stable her if you'd rather. Our fields are bigger than a lot of ponies are used to, so if you think she'll be difficult to catch —"

"No, she's always easy," I said quickly.

"Millie will show you where, then. We've checked that all the horses have their vaccinations and worming up-to-date – just like Jade – so you're all set."

I'd taken all my pony's travel gear off and now she walked beside me, keeping level with my shoulder and looking around her with great interest.

"She's amazing," Millie seemed very relaxed and chatty. "My boy, Chas, was a complete lunatic when we unloaded him, all wild-eyed and panicky. I put him in a stable first, but Zak said to put him in the field and he'll soon calm down, and he did."

"I met Zak just now," I said, waiting while Millie unlatched another gate. "He was going somewhere on Jet, and said he wouldn't be long."

"Yeah, well I'll believe that when I see it," Millie said cryptically. "He's gone off to see Tasha, so he could be a long time."

"Tasha?"

"His girlfriend," she gave a deep sigh. "Good-looking of course, but a total pain."

I didn't quite know how to respond to that so I said lamely, "Oh, right."

"You'd think, wouldn't you, that a gorgeous guy like Zak would have the most perfect girlfriend in the universe but – oh, here we are. I'll get the gate again."

We'd arrived at the well-fenced perimeter of a huge field that stretched away to a line of trees in the distance. The grass looked good; there were two big, clean water troughs and about eight horses grazed contentedly in a group off to our right.

"It's OK, I'll do it, thanks," I slid the latch and walked Jade through, getting her to stand politely as I shut it again.

I'd have liked to do our kiss and cuddle routine but knew I'd feel pretty self-conscious in front of a new acquaintance, so I took off her head collar right away and waited. She blew gently into my face, her velvet nose brushing my skin.

"Your vacation starts now, baby," I whispered and she gave me a last affectionate nudge before moving away.

"Chas dragged me nearly halfway across the field. He couldn't wait to get out there," Millie was impressed.

"Jade always likes to say goodbye," I watched intently as my pony approached the other horses.

A rangy looking chestnut raised his head and surveyed her, whinnying loudly.

"That's my Chas," Millie hopped onto the fence to watch. "Oh, and there's Fenton. He looks interested too."

The iron gray Fenton was the first to reach Jade, standing in front of her and arching his neck. She tossed her head and they breathed in each other's smells as they stood quietly nose-to-nose. Now Chas wanted to join in

20

so he pranced close and whinnied once more. Jade tossed her head again, sending her glossy black mane flying as she took off in a perfect extended canter. Chas plunged and cavorted, following eagerly, but it was the gray horse that joined her, cantering close alongside. The excitement spread to the other horses and for a few minutes they galloped together across the open expanse of grass like a flock of birds reveling in the freedom of the skies. They looked absolutely stunning, and Jade, at their head, was a poem of movement, every turn, twist and spin performed with style and grace. Soon they were slowing, the exuberant gallop becoming a canter, the wide, curving circles diminishing until the display petered out and the herd regrouped and settled. I saw Jade's nose drop to inspect the ground and then she too was happily grazing, all her concentration focused on cropping the short, sweet grass.

"Look at Fenton. He couldn't get much closer if he tried," Millie laughed and pointed to the dark gray head right next to Jade's pretty bay one.

"Who does Fenton belong to?" I asked, not taking my eyes off my pony. "Is he one of the Beacon Lodge horses?"

"No, he's a guest horse. His owner's named Tom and he was here last year too. Tom and Fenton are totally the best at Pony Club games. They can win at practically every game ever invented!"

"Oh," I felt a little stupid telling her Jade and I had never even tried mounted games. "Are you and Chas good at that too?"

"We're not much good at anything, to be honest." Millie said frankly. "Show jumping's our best bet unless it's against the clock."

"Why, what happens then?" I laughed at her expression.

"Sheer chaos," she said, making another face. "Chas gets so excited he forgets everything he's ever been taught and I lose all control so we end up hurtling around the ring like a runaway express train. I suppose you and Jade are great at everything – you've sort of got that partnership look when you're together."

"Thanks," I hesitated, still feeling a little shy. "We've done some jumping, but haven't entered many competitions so I don't know if we're any good."

"Oh you'll soon find out. Zak organizes mini shows for us, and Ed and Val are great teachers so anything you're not good at they'll soon fix."

"Sounds good," I said, feeling that buzz of excitement again as I watched Jade settle in so beautifully and listened to Millie's entertaining, upbeat chat. "The thing I'm really looking forward to is swimming in the sea. I bet Jade is going to absolutely love it."

"Yeah? I thought that about Chas but it took nearly a week to get him in. He'd wade but he wouldn't go any deeper."

"How did you persuade him in the end?"

"Zak did it. We go to the beach practically every day and he just persevered, encouraging us a little further each time, till suddenly there we were – swimming!"

"It looks amazing," I said with feeling. "I saw the picture on the website and –"

"Hey that's us – Chas and me!" She slid off the fence and struck a pose. "The two horses swimming in the picture are Chas and Fenton! Ed took the photo last year. I've got a copy on my bedroom wall – it's a terrific one of Zak, isn't it?"

"I didn't notice," I said honestly. "Was he one of the riders cantering through the surf?"

"You didn't – duh!" Millie stared at me in disbelief. "I bet Zak is the reason most girls book to come here. Don't you think he's totally gorgeous?"

"He _is_ cute," I agreed cautiously. "But he's definitely not why _I'm_ here."

"You must be nuts," she flopped to the grass and fanned herself dramatically with one hand. "Zak is so gorgeous he's practically edible!"

"I'll take your word for it," I sat down next to her, still keeping a close eye on Jade. "He's way too old for me, and anyway what about the beautiful girlfriend? Tasha, right? She must cramp everyone's style."

"She's all right. In fact she can be fun sometimes, but she's high maintenance – what's known as fiery. Which in my book means she's just plain argumentative."

"Not so good," I said, a bit nervously. "I don't like arguing with people so I think I'll try avoiding her. She doesn't actually work at Beacon Lodge, does she?"

"Well, she's at college, a drama student, which figures. But that means she's on vacation now, so she helps out here, mainly because Zak wants her around all the time."

"He must be pretty sweet on her," I said, getting bored with the subject. "So, while we're here would you tell me the names of all the horses we can see, Millie?"

"I don't know them all. There are three other new guests besides you this time."

I sat up as Jade moved across the field and another bay lifted his head to look at her. "Who's that one?"

"Dunno. Your horse is _fine_, Caitlin, you don't need to worry. We could leave her now, you know."

"I'll just give it another five minutes or so," I looked at her apologetically. "Sorry, I'm just a – little –"

"Nuts about Jade?" She grinned at me. "Don't worry, I totally get it. OK, I'll tell you the names I know – that palomino mare for instance – she's Sabrina and she belongs to Tasha. The light gray gelding is Peter and he's Ed's, and the chubby roan is Val's horse, Rusty. I think I heard Zak say the piebald one is Lucas and there's a girl who sounded a little sappy, going on and on about her darling Teddy, so one of them is named that."

"Unless she was talking about a stuffed toy," I suggested, not very wittily.

Millie was nice enough to laugh. "Could be. Corinne, that's the girl's name, and she's probably all right but I didn't take to her. You know how it is sometimes."

I felt flattered since she seemed to have 'taken' to me, and said self-consciously that we could go now if she liked.

"It's OK," she yawned and stretched out on the grass. "I'm not in a hurry till Zak's around. He usually takes us all across the cliffs for our first ride so we can look down at the beach and across the countryside. Last year he rode real close to me because Chas got so excited that Zak was worried my loopy horse would fall off the cliff."

"Real close?" I teased her. "Is that when you realized Zak was the perfect man?"

"Don't knock it, just you wait! I bet within twenty-four hours you'll be feeling just like I do."

"No chance," I stood up and stretched, giving Jade one last, careful scrutiny. "Maybe we should get back and meet up with the others."

"If you want," she said amiably, rolling over and getting to her feet. "They'll be in the yard. I'll show you."

The other four were, indeed, lolling around in a shady part of the pretty yard and they greeted us in friendly fashion.

"Sorry, I don't know everybody's names, just Tom from last year, but I'm Millie and this is Caitlin," my new friend helped herself to a cold drink from a tray.

"Hi Caitlin." Tom, tall and blond, handed me a glass. "Millie might have gotten to meet everyone properly if she hadn't shot off to find Zak as soon as she arrived. Anyway, this is Corinne, Andy and Jacob."

We all murmured hello and how ya doing and I wondered if anyone else felt as shy and nervous as I did.

"So Caitlin, are you new to this like me?" Corinne, who at fifteen and a half was a few months older than the rest of us, was pretty in a Barbie Doll kind of way.

"New?" I gaped a bit stupidly. "Um no, I've had Jade nearly five years and was riding about a year before that."

"No I mean new to Beacon Lodge," she spoke s-l-o-w-l-y and clearly, obviously thinking I was pretty dumb. "I realize we're all experienced riders. Andy here is an ace at cross country, for instance, and once he reaches sixteen he'll be in advanced."

"Oh really?" I said lamely. "I'm not advanced at anything, I'm afraid."

"Doesn't matter," Tom said easily. "Beacon Lodge is mainly for fun, though Val and Ed are great at teaching competitive riding if you want it."

"Caitlin just wants to swim in the ocean with her pony," Millie said through a mouthful of potato chips.

"Yeah, I can't wait to do that too." Jacob, the shortest of the three guys moved in close. "Maybe Caitlin and I could go to the beach while you others are working on your jumping."

"We ride down to the ocean practically every day anyway," Tom said mildly. "It'll be more fun for Caitlin in a group."

"Yeah, I'd like that," I smiled at him gratefully, slightly freaked out by Jacob's over-eagerness. "And anyway, I want to improve my show jumping. Jade's great at it and I don't want to hold her back."

"Jade's a pretty name," Corinne said brightly. "What color is she?"

"Bay," I said, then, feeling that was a bit abrupt, added, "A light bay with jet black mane and tail."

"Oh, like my Teddy," she enthused and I tried hard not to look at Millie who was grinning wickedly.

"How were all the horses when you checked?" Andy asked her. "Blaze settled down the minute I turned him out, couldn't believe it."

"Yeah, they were all great. They ran around a little when Caitlin put Jade in the field, but we stayed and watched for while –"

"And they were all fine," I put in hastily, not wanting her to tell them how obsessively I'd watched my pony.

I was surprised how comfortable it was chatting with them all. I've never found it easy being part of a group but the fact the conversation was all about horses made it more natural than usual for me to join in. We chilled out for another half an hour or so and I felt myself starting to relax and enjoy their company, even finding the very girly Corinne and slightly intense Jacob were no problem. By the time Ed came over to see us there was a lot of laughing going on and his broad smile became even wider.

"You seem like a happy group," he commented. "How about a guided tour? Or is that too serious?"

"A tour would be good," Jacob said, jumping up immediately, but Millie waved a lazy hand.

"Nah. I already know this place like the back of my hand."

"OK," Ed said, winking at us. "The rest of you come and meet Zak. He'll be the one showing you around."

"Oh all right then," Millie grumbled, trying unsuccessfully to look cool. "I might as well join in."

She somehow managed to sidle around Corinne and get right next to Zak as he took us around the fabulous grounds, showing us the impressive school, the beautiful area containing a scary looking cross country course, and some of the outbuildings and trails.

"You've all been shown your rooms and the rest of the house, right?" Zak's teeth flashed white in the good-looking face.

"Uh, no I haven't." I realized I didn't even know where my backpack was. "I just settled Jade in the field and then hung out in the yard."

"Sorry Caitlin," he moved quickly to my side. "Your bag's been taken to your room. I'll show you where."

As we started walking up the stairs he stopped and took something from the hall table. "I'd better put this back in the office upstairs where it belongs. It's my dad's favorite paperweight. Look, there's a real sea horse inside."

I glanced briefly at the ornament, more interested in looking around me. The house was nice, cool and airy, and to my delight my bedroom window had a view of the paddock.

"Fantastic!" I leaned out blissfully. "I can see Jade first thing in the morning. There she is – look."

Zak craned his neck to see, squashed up so close beside me in the window that I could smell the clean scent of his skin.

"She's terrific," his brilliant blue eyes smiled into mine. "I can't wait to see you two together."

It must have been the excitement of beginning this vacation, I reasoned later, that made my insides perform a sudden, ecstatic lurch. I mean, what else could possibly have made me feel an emotion so strong, glorious and completely unexpected?

CHAPTER THREE

I didn't have any time to think about it; within seconds
Zak had moved away and was leaving the room.

"I'm taking a short ride across the cliffs in half an
hour," he turned at the door. "So if you want to come
along get your riding gear unpacked."

"Oh, yes please," I said, sounding slightly breathless
even to me. "Um, see you in the yard then."

"Great," he gave one more teeth flashing grin and
disappeared.

Feeling distinctly light headed I unpacked my
backpack, got into my riding pants, and put all my other
stuff away in cupboards and drawers. Then I re-braided
my long hair, checked my appearance in the mirror
(twice) and went downstairs carrying boots and hat.
Tom was in the boot room and gave what I thought was
a sarcastic wolf whistle when I walked in. I ignored him
and, hearing Millie's voice outside, backed out again.

"Hi Caitlin," she grinned at me cheerfully. "You look
good. I wish I had legs up to my armpits like that!"

"Funn*ee*," I said, tweaking her spiky bangs. "I was
pretty sure you'd be on this ride, seeing that Zak's taking
us out."

"You bet," she rolled her eyes and pretended to
swoon. "With a little luck Chas will act up again and Zak
will have to rescue me."

"You might get *really* lucky and it could even be me doing the rescuing." A grinning Andy squeezed past us, followed by Jacob.

"Where's Corinne?" I asked as we all tugged our boots on.

"She's lying down, tired out from the journey here," Tom said, waiting by the door. "Come *on,* you guys."

We walked out together to the paddock where the others started plodding their way over to the group of grazing horses. I stayed near the gate and gave one long, low whistle, watching with pleasure as Jade's head came up immediately. I whistled again and she began moving toward me, her trot quickly becoming a canter.

"Look at that," Millie said as she stopped and stared. "Caitlin's horse can't wait to be with her!"

"Oh fantastic, she's bringing mine too!" Tom cheered as the iron gray Fenton followed my pony, breaking eagerly into a fast trot to try and keep up with her.

Soon he, too, was cantering and when Jade slowed and stopped in front of me, Fenton slithered to an ungainly halt as well.

"Thanks, pal, you just saved me a walk," Tom slipped a rope around his horse's neck. "Lucky for me you've got good taste in women!"

"He's definitely fallen for my girl, hasn't he?" I gave Jade a welcoming cuddle and turned toward the gate. "He's been following her around ever since she arrived."

"I hope she's happy with that." For a moment Tom's gray eyes were serious but then they widened. "Jade's just walking beside you, no head collar, no nothing!"

"I don't really need one for her," I unlatched the gate and walked through with my pony at my side.

She turned neatly to wait while Tom and Fenton went through and then nudged the gate shut as I'd taught her.

"Phew!" Tom said, really impressed. "Does she put her own saddle and bridle on as well?"

"Not yet, but I'm working on it," I grinned and we walked up to the yard, laughing and joking.

By the time the other three joined us with their horses we'd brushed, polished and picked out our horses' feet and were waiting with saddles ready, showing off. Zak rode in on the gleaming Jet and I heard a wistful intake of breath from Millie when she saw him.

"OK?" He grinned at us. "I think we'll have Caitlin and Jade next to me, followed by Jacob on Lucas then Andy with Blaze while you two old timers bring up the rear, Millie, since you know your way around so well."

I saw Millie's face fall and gave her an apologetic smile before moving Jade to ride alongside the black Thoroughbred. Zak opened the main gate with a remote control and we moved off along the driveway where long shadows fell across the grass from the late afternoon sun. It was still warm and a gentle breeze lifted the horses' manes a little as we turned left to follow a grassy trail. This wound its way through some small woods, then climbed fairly sharply up the cliff side, the turf beneath us still short and springy, perfect for riding. Once the horses were warmed up Zak, sitting lightly in the saddle with the wonderfully arrogant ease of a born rider, moved Jet from a trot into a working canter. Jade, enjoying herself as usual, tried to plunge with him but I held her until I was ready, giving the smallest of touches to produce her free striding pace. Taking her up to join the black horse, I kept her in line with his handsome head, loving the exhilarating feeling of speed and tasting the first salty tang of sea breeze. We cantered the long length of the slope and I could feel Jade buzzing with excitement as she too breathed in the exotic new flavor of the coastal air.

And then we were there. The ground beneath us leveled, the ocean was stretched before us, and the silver tinsel of every ripple turned to gold as the sun began its descent. The air was filled with the evocative sound of seagulls crying and the glorious crash of waves breaking on the rocks below. Zak reined his horse in and we sat taking in the spectacular sweep of the bay, its rocky, smoke colored cliffs towering above the pale stretch of sand. Millie, her mind obviously not on the breathtaking scenery, walked Chas over to join us.

"Nice, eh?" She grinned at me meaningfully, nodding surreptitiously toward Zak. "The view, I mean."

"It's – it's stunning," I said honestly.

"Look, Caitlin," Zak said, leaning forward. "Over there, a fishing boat coming home."

I tried to focus and he bent nearer, pointing in the right direction. "There, see?"

We were almost as close as we'd been in the window and I positively *felt* Millie bristle.

"Got it!" I moved quickly away, leaving her and Chas next to him.

Slightly shaken, I suppose I wasn't concentrating and when a particularly vocal seagull swooped suddenly, making Jade spook, I just wasn't ready. Jade, used to the instant reaction of my calming hand, and fired up with the excitement of this wonderful new landscape, shied naughtily, throwing me off balance. The reins slid from my

33

fingers, I lost both stirrups and suddenly she was plunging forward completely out of control. I pulled myself together at once and would have regained my grip, my seat and my poise but Zak was quicker. He raced alongside to grab the reins and bring us to a halt, only a few feet, I have to admit, from the edge of the towering cliff.

"Sorry!" I gasped and he smiled directly into my eyes.

"It's OK, don't worry."

My hair had come loose from its braid and flowed in a dark mass around my shoulders and I knew my eyes were huge as I stared, mesmerized, back at him. Convinced that I looked like some kind of startled Bambi I dropped my gaze and turned away, feeling bewildered and confused.

"You all right, Caitlin?" Tom's nice, kind face was concerned.

"Yes, thanks. It was my own stupid fault – I wasn't concentrating."

We moved on, keeping well away from the cliff edge and at a sedate walking pace. I was furious with myself and tried to stay at the back, out of everyone's way, but Zak insisted I stay next to him.

"He probably thinks I'm a nervous little novice rider incapable of keeping her pony under control," I told myself bitterly. "And now I've spoiled the first ride out for everyone else as well!"

I beat myself up about it the whole time we were out, not even cheering up when Zak pointed down to the beautiful beach we'd be swimming from.

"We've got some work ahead of us in the morning – we thought Pony Club games would be a good ice breaker – then we're going down there tomorrow

afternoon. You'll have your first-ever swimming lesson with Jade. That'll be good won't it, Caitlin?"

I grunted a yes but wouldn't look at him, feeling more and more naive and stupid with every minute. For the first time ever I couldn't wait to finish a ride, and got Jade back into the paddock in record time. There was a choice of games or a movie to watch after we'd eaten, but I just couldn't lift myself out of my black mood and took off upstairs on my own. I woke really early and lay in bed for a few minutes, listening to the bird song and watching the room gradually lighten as the sun came up. I felt better. The inexplicable bad temper had left me and, though ashamed of myself, I was sure I could put the silly incident behind me and move on.

The first thing I did was open the curtains and look out at the paddock, my heart lifting even further when I saw Jade contentedly grazing. Her new friend Fenton was close beside her again and I thought, not for the first time, how much better at getting on with life she was than I am. I dressed and left the house quietly, entering the field and spending over an hour just being with my pony. After a while she lay on the grass beside me, closing her eyes blissfully as I stroked and petted her. I told her what a fool I thought I'd made of myself the day before, going on and on about it until she fell asleep, snoring gently with her head in my lap.

"You're making too big a deal of it, you know," Tom's approach had been so quiet I hadn't heard him behind me. "It was nothing. No one else was bothered – well that's not exactly true, I guess."

"Oh?" I looked at him, still feeling embarrassed. "Zak, I suppose? He must think I'm a totally inept moron."

36

"I bet not. Zak's seen a million guest riders and I'd put money on you being a lot better than most."

"Yeah?" I said, finding I really, *really* wanted Zak to approve of me. "Who's mad about me messing up?"

"Millie. She thinks you set up your little adventure so you could bat your big brown eyes and get all the attention from her beloved Zak."

"No way!" I couldn't believe it. "As if I'd deliberately make myself look a complete idiot!"

"You miss the point," he said, not looking at me. "She thinks you did it to make Zak notice you."

"Oh no!" I groaned. "It's *Millie* who's totally gaga about him, not me. And if I wanted someone to notice me I'd find a better way of doing it than making a complete fool of myself. And as for putting Jade in danger like that –"

Words failed me and I saw Tom's shoulders relax. "Just tell her that then, and she'll soon calm down. She's a nice kid. A little bit of a flake sometimes, especially where Lover Boy's concerned, but she's mostly all right."

I hesitated. "From what you just said I take it you're not that impressed with Zak yourself?"

"Don't mind me, I'm just jealous – the guy has every female within miles swooning at him so the rest of us are bound to feel a bit resentful. Zak's OK, really."

"I'll fix things with Millie," I promised. "I'm sorry I didn't handle it very well yesterday. I don't know what was the matter with me."

"Maybe you were jetlagged like Corinne," he said lightly, leaning over to pat the still sleeping Jade.

She opened one eye and saw him, getting immediately to her feet.

"Sorry," Tom smiled at me ruefully. "Now I've gone and spoiled your cuddle."

"We'll have plenty more." I stroked my pony with one hand and slid the other around Fenton who, as usual, was very close by. "Hello, you."

The gray pony snorted amiably and nuzzled Jade's neck.

"He's got it bad," again Tom didn't look at me. "I just hope she feels the same way."

"Do we take them into the yard yet," I asked, "or is it still too early?"

He looked at his watch. "Yeah, a little. We should go and have breakfast first, I think."

It was a cheerful, impromptu meal with all six of us helping ourselves from a selection of cereals, toast and fruit while Val cooked eggs and stuff in the kitchen. Corinne, looking refreshed and pretty glamorous with full makeup and immaculate hair, was nibbling at some toast while Andy and Jacob sat beside her wolfing down king-sized omelets. Millie was there too, piling up a dish with fresh apricots and bananas. She saw me come in and her expression changed immediately.

"Hi," I walked toward her. "Can I join you?"

She tossed her head in theatrical fashion and turned up her nose. "No thanks."

"Oh come on Millie," I lowered my voice. "I'm really sorry I annoyed you yesterday, but it was an accident, I swear. I'm not after Zak, not at all, honestly."

"Yeah right," she turned her back and went over to the window, as far away as she could.

I followed. "Jade spooks occasionally. She's not perfect and she can be a naughty mare sometimes. I wasn't concentrating – if I had been I'd have stopped her on my own, but Zak was just quicker, that's all."

"Don't give me that," she said, really upset. "I saw the way you looked at him, and I'd already told you how to keep him real close. You really went for it, didn't you, shaking your hair all loose and giving him the wide eyed, 'Oh Zak, you're my hero' treatment."

"You've got it all wrong." I pushed away the memory of the tremor Zak's proximity had sent surging through my body. "I was shaken up, that's all, and let's face it, I must have looked stupid, gaping at him like a fish."

"You weren't flirting?" she looked at me warily. "All that hair tossing and stuff?"

"The elastic band on my braid broke," I said impatiently. "And I might not know much about flirting but I think acting like a total jerk isn't one of the best ways to do it!"

"You were dead quiet afterwards," poor Millie said, still unconvinced. "Zak was concerned. He kept coming over and trying to talk to you."

"He was just doing his job," I said wearily. "Making sure the customers are happy, that's all."

"Yeah," she gave a small smile. "And you don't think he's gorgeous?"

"He's all right," I said cagily. "But he's like *years* older than me, and he's got a girlfriend, so he's not even worth a second thought."

"That doesn't stop me from liking him," she said, her lip quivering, but then she brightened suddenly. "But, hey, I bet he's fallen out with Tasha! She didn't come over last night and he didn't go over there."

"Maybe he's dumped her." I wanted Millie to be happy again.

39

"Yeah and it's about time too!" The smile was back in place. "So, you having any breakfast or what?"

I laughed and went to get some, and then we sat with Tom, soon recapturing the easy familiarity of the previous day.

"OK," Tom said, pushing away his plate and standing up. "Let's go and bring in those horses and get them ready for a games contest!"

To my surprise I wasn't that nervous when, warmed up and ready, we rode into the small field Zak had prepared for the morning session. All the other riders had done at least *some* Pony Club games so I'd expected to feel awkward and novicey but they were all so laid back about my lack of experience that it made me relax too. He started off with a demonstration of techniques – stuff I'd seen before from the sideline at shows but never really concentrated on. Zak asked Jade and me to stand alongside him so he could explain exactly what was going on. Millie shot me a suspicious look as I moved across to join him but I made a clown face at her and mouthed, "No way – he's all yours remember!" Zak was really good at describing the games the others showed me, breaking down each movement so I'd understand its usage.

"Watch Tom now, Caitlin," he said. We were several feet apart, intently studying the action. "The first team to finish always wins, so to save precious seconds Tom will vault onto Fenton's back while the horse is moving – watch the stages. First he runs alongside with his left hand holding the reins on top of Fenton's neck, his right hand grasping the saddle on the far side. Then he pushes off with both feet, springing upwards with his weight supported on his right arm. A smooth swing of the right leg and he's in the saddle, shortening reins, settling and gaining control all before his pony's completed two strides."

"I can do that!" I said excitedly. "I ride Jade bareback and that's exactly how I – what's he doing now?"

"It's called a pyramid race, still fast and furious but the horse must stand perfectly still to allow each rider to stack up the pyramid – whoops, Millie let Chas rush past and the whole thing's toppled over!"

I laughed with him, turning my head to look into his face, and as I did so Tom called out, "Look, there's Tasha – she's coming over!"

Zak's eyes swung straight to the approaching rider and I clearly saw the look of adoration in their brilliant blue depths. There was absolutely no doubt about the way he felt about his girlfriend and, unfortunately for me, I was also sure about the emotion that was coursing through my own being. For the first time in my life I was jealous, with an intensity that almost startled me into blurting out exactly how I felt.

CHAPTER FOUR

Luckily, I managed to keep my mouth clamped shut and watched silently as Zak rode his horse across the field to meet Tasha. He leaned forward and kissed her mouth lightly and I saw her smile. She was about nineteen and beautiful, of course, slim but curvy, and the dark red hair pulled casually back from her delicate face rippled almost to her waist. Andy and Jacob were gaping at her in delight, tongues practically hanging out, and even Tom, who'd seen her before, looked mildly stunned.

"Hiyah," she called, bringing her pretty palomino mare over to join us. "I'm Tasha – I promise I'll learn all your names as we go along."

"You already know mine," Millie said chirpily. "And Tom. We were here last year, remember? We're doing Pony Club games today, and only Caitlin hasn't done it before."

"Oh right," Tasha had a great smile and I tried not to notice the besotted way Zak was looking at her.

I thought it was just as well I was about to learn a whole batch of new techniques that I was going to need for competition games. It would give me a chance to pull myself together. I'd never had a crush on anyone before but I had to recognize I had a *gigantic* one now. The breathless, swoony feeling I'd experienced twice the day before had nothing to do with the excitement of starting a vacation or the fact Jade had spooked out on the ride. It was being close to Zak Meadows that had caused it and the illogical, spiteful surge of jealousy had been directed at his girlfriend simply because she *was* his girlfriend! Before I could analyze the situation into a horrible muddle, I had to get on with the job confronting me, which was riding a by now very hyped-up and excited Jade in our first ever Pony Club game.

"A simple one to start with," Zak said. "It's called Musical Mats."

The concept certainly wasn't rocket science. We all cantered in a circle around old sacks laid out on the ground while music played. Tasha was in charge of a radio and when she switched it off we had to dismount and, leading our ponies, get to one of the sack "mats" and stand on it. It was very straightforward, I thought as I put Jade into a canter behind Tom and Fenton. We rode two complete circuits, and the music stopped. I slid off and started jogging toward the nearest mat – only to see Tom step quickly onto it.

"Come on Jade," running faster, I headed off for the next nearest, nearly reaching it before Corinne, who, panting slightly, jumped onto the middle of it. I looked around wildly – everyone else was also standing on a mat, smugly holding their ponies' reins. Sprinting now, I hurtled around the circle to the last remaining sack, but just as I placed a foot on it Jade, obviously not understanding the game at all, kept going, taking me with her. By digging my heels in the ground, leaning against her shoulder and shouting, "Whoa, Jade, *whoa*!" I eventually stopped her and plodded back to stand on the mat, shaking my head apologetically to the others who were all doubled over laughing.

"OK," Zak was grinning too, "This time we take one of the mats away, so you'll have to be a lot quicker, Caitlin."

I tried not to think how gorgeous he looked and nodded. We're fast learners, Jade and me, and by the third round of music we were really competing, in a smooth rhythm of canter, halt, dismount, run. Millie was the first to be eliminated, choosing the same mat as Andy who outran her easily. Next to go was Jacob who slid off his piebald pony's back so fast he fell over before he could even start running.

"I don't mind too much," he said, gazing up at us ruefully. "But Lucas couldn't care less that we're out – look at him!"

The black and white cob had simply taken the opportunity to start grazing, practically stepping over his rider on the way. I was beginning to feel fired up; the strong competitive spirit I knew existed flared into a definite spark within me. There were now only three mats and four of us playing, and the second the music stopped I flung myself out of the saddle and sprinted to the nearest mat, Jade trotting at my shoulder. I made it onto the mat a fraction of a second before Corinne arrived with Teddy and grinned at her triumphantly.

"That's not fair," she said instantly. "Caitlin's not holding her horse's reins."

"Jade's right here next to me though," I defended myself.

"It's not in the rules," Corinne said, sticking out her lower lip. "Is it, Zak?"

He shrugged helplessly. "I've never seen anyone do it like that, but Caitlin's right – she's on the mat and her horse is with her."

"I think the rules say you have to *lead* your pony," Tasha said. "But no one made that clear so you can't eliminate Caitlin, and it was fantastic the way Jade followed her."

"Yeah, but if it's not in the rules –" Corinne persisted.

Then Andy suggested quickly, "Let's do it again, but this time Caitlin has to lead her horse like the rest of us."

"Seems fair," Zak said, smiling at me. "Is it OK with you?"

"Sure," I stepped off the mat and remounted.

This time the music played for over three circuits before Tasha, with her back to us so she couldn't see our positions, switched it off. I ran like the wind, with Jade's reins hooked over one finger, and reached the mat safely. Corinne had gone for the same one as Tom and he beat her to it easily, standing on its center with his arms folded.

"Tough luck, Corinne," Zak said easily and she smiled at him, unable to resist that fabulous combination of blue eyes and white teeth.

I climbed back up again, thinking wryly that it looked as if I was going to have to join the club when it came to being smitten by Zak! I concentrated on the game, trying to shave nanoseconds off my time as I sprang from the saddle, but the guys were faster, claiming the last two mats way before I did, leaving me eliminated. Tom went on to win and got a round of applause as his reward.

"Are you all getting into the spirit of the thing?" Zak's eyes were twinkling. "Because now you're going to compete as a team. Divide yourselves into two teams of three and come on over here."

To my surprise Tom moved purposefully toward me. "Will you be on my team, Caitlin?"

"Oh yeah," I said, flattered. "But I'm terrible – I don't know a thing."

"You're a natural," he said. "So who else should we get?"

"'Fraid you've got me," Millie said in a small voice. "Andy, Jacob and Corinne have already teamed up."

"Great." Tom was incredibly good-natured, not seeming to mind getting the two novices at all. "Let's see what the first game is."

It was a flag race, the first team rider galloping across the field to plant a flag into a bucket, then racing back to the start so the second could take off and place his flag and so on. Tom was the first to go from our team, flying across the grass with Fenton looking like a steel gray arrow. He barely slowed as they curved around the bucket, leaning out of the saddle to drop the flag neatly while single-handedly guiding his horse in a smooth canter, then picking up the pace for the gallop back. Millie and Chas took off like a rocket and they were ahead of Jacob in the other team when she reached the end, but she had to slow the over-anxious Chas right down before she could place her flag, allowing Jacob's piebald pony to catch up. They were neck and neck as they raced back and Jade and I took off just a fraction after Corinne and Teddy.

My wonderful pony is fast though, and we'd pulled ahead and were leading by two strides as I neck reined her around the bucket. Trying too hard, I stood up in the stirrups and dropped my flag from a height. It landed squarely and accurately but before I could complete our turn and race triumphantly back, the bucket tottered and swayed, tipping out the three flags and rolling across the grass. I threw myself to the ground and gathered up the flags, sticking them back in and returning the upright bucket to its proper place but of course I'd wasted tons of time. Corinne had placed her flag safely and was already half way back to her teammates – we'd lost.

"I'm sorry," I wailed as Jade and I cantered back. "I completely blew it."

"Don't worry about it – we'll get them next time," Tom promised.

That wasn't quite true. During the next game Millie lost the lead Tom had given us when Chas shied, but after that we just scraped a win in the hectic bending contest. Another marginal victory for us in the more sedate egg and spoon race meant the two teams were tied.

"We'll do the 'bride and groom' race as a decider," Zak announced. "It's designed for teams of four so I'll join Tom's side and Tasha will be on Andy's."

I saw Andy and Jacob's faces light up immediately at the thought of being joined by Tasha while Millie was practically dancing because she'd be with Zak. It was a fast and furious game involving a lot of vaulting so we all had a few minutes practice beforehand. Millie and I stood on a line way across the field waiting for our "grooms" to rescue us. Zak came first, galloping on the stunning black Jet and Millie, trembling with excitement, sprang lightly up behind him. A curving turn and they were galloping back to the start with Millie curled blissfully against Zak. Once they crossed the line Tom and Fenton were off, hurtling flat out toward us. As I'd told Zak, I've been happily vaulting onto Jade's back for years but I'd never done it at this speed and certainly never swung up behind another rider this way. Tom knew I was worrying and

slowed his horse's pace, helping to steady me as I leapt
up and across Fenton's back.

"That was good," I panted as I slid to the ground at the
finish. "But you don't need to slow it down so much. I
can do it, I know I can."

"Good for you, Caitlin," Zak grinned at me. "You're a
real competitor. It comes naturally to you."

We had a few more practice vaults, and then Zak
called the two teams together and set the contest up
for real. Millie, Corinne and I set off across the field,
accompanied by Tasha.

"You're doing really well," she smiled at me, tossing
back her long switch of hair. "And so are you, Millie.
You and Chas are ten times better than last year. I know
Zak thinks so."

"*Does* he?" Millie's eyes were glowing and I thought
uneasily that Tasha would realize how smitten the
younger girl was.

"Don't get carried away, Millie," Corinne said sharply.
"Zak just told *me* how well I was doing too."

"I'm sure he thinks highly of all of you," Tasha said
easily. "OK, here we are. Get ready to be rescued, girls!
Who's going first?"

"Me," Millie said at once. "If that's all right with you,
Caitlin?"

"Sure," I knew how much she enjoyed cuddling into
Zak. "I'll wait back here for my turn."

Tasha and I moved out of the way, making sure we
left plenty of room for the first two "grooms" on their
galloping horses. Squinting back at the start I was
surprised to see Tom lining up first for our team and I
heard Zak's voice shout, "One – two – three – GO!"

Fenton and Blaze sprang immediately into action with Tom heading straight for Millie while Andy went flat out toward Corinne. The teams were neck and neck, both girls vaulting expertly behind the two riders as the horses curved around to gallop back down the field. Tasha and I ran back to the "bride" places, both poised and ready. Zak and Jet started slightly behind Jacob on the piebald Lucas but they made up the difference with ease and had pulled ahead when they reached me. I misjudged my leap slightly so that Zak had to check his horse, taking a wider turn before we started on the return ride. Tasha, athletic and graceful, performed a perfect spring, enabling Jacob to regain the lead and they were several yards ahead, galloping strongly to the finish line. Curved against Zak's strong, muscular body, I felt Jet surge forward, his long, powerful stride eating up the ground beneath us until we were alongside the piebald. Tasha's beautiful hair streamed out behind her and she was laughing as we passed. I saw the wicked, conspiratorial grin Zak gave her and when we came to a triumphant halt the first thing he did was go over and hug her. I stayed with Jet, stroking his gleaming shoulder and trying not to look at the laughing, happy couple.

"Well *done*, Caitlin," Zak took his horse's reins and patted my shoulder casually. "I went all out for that win and you coped really well."

I mumbled something about not getting it quite right but now Millie had joined us and she was saying nice things too.

"You're already better than I am, and I've been practicing for a whole year," Millie ended ruefully.

"Um – sorry about you not getting Zak that time," I

kept my voice low. "I thought he was riding the first run, not Tom."

"It's OK, so did I," she said, sighing theatrically. "Isn't he just *fabulous*?"

"Uh – yes, he's a terrific rider," I said cautiously. "Did you see the way we went past poor old Lucas?"

"Yeah, and Zak was flirting with Tasha at the time," Millie said, sighing again. "They're so lovey dovey, those two, it makes you sick."

"You don't seem to mind her though," I said, still experiencing shameful pangs of jealousy, as though someone was turning a knife between my ribs, every time Zak and Tasha were together. Millie must be a lot more sensible than I am, I thought, or maybe she's just plain nicer.

"There's no point in minding, is there?" she said cheerfully. "Let's face it, Zak's never going to choose me instead of her, but I can dream, can't I?"

I smiled at her, wondering whether to tell her I was totally knocked out by the good-looking Zak too.

"I just live in hope that Tasha's temper will get the better of her during our vacation," Millie went on. "It would be just perfect if I became the only girl here who felt that way about him."

I opened my mouth to say that wouldn't be the case, then closed it again. I really liked Millie; she was so upbeat and buoyant and she seemed to like me too, so I didn't want to ruin our budding friendship by spoiling her daydreams.

"How you doing, teammates?" Tom had brought our horses over. "*Victorious* teammates, I should say."

"Well, good. I enjoyed it, thanks," I smiled at him. "Though I'm going to need a lot more practice."

51

"I'll give you a hand if you like," he swung into his saddle. "Your horse could be a real star at this, you're already so in tune with each other."

"Thanks, but maybe I'm not so good with people! Is Corinne still mad at me?"

"Nah, she's fine. She's just one of those fussy types. She's got Andy and Jacob running around after her, so she's pretty happy."

"Really?" I looked over to where the other team was still in a huddle. "I thought they were both sweet on Tasha."

"Apples to oranges. Tasha's way out of their league – it's like Millie liking Zak. It's never going to happen. Look, the bending poles are still in place. D'you want another try at them?"

"Yeah." I liked the fact that while I was riding I had to concentrate, and therefore stop thinking about Zak.

As we moved across the field I saw Ed walk onto the field.

"He'll watch us all practicing but he won't get involved," Tom explained. "He and Val do all the proper riding, from dressage to cross country, but they leave Zak in charge of mounted games."

"If you want extra help, stick with Tom," Millie advised, riding past. "I need Zak to help me."

"He's all yours," I said lightly, proud of the way I was hiding my feelings.

It was better being with Tom anyway because I felt comfortable with him and didn't feel all self conscious and useless like I did when I was trying to impress Zak. Tom helped me improve my vaulting technique and showed Jade and me how to speed up in the bending.

"She loves it," I said, slowing my pony after her brilliant display of snaking between the poles. "I bet she could do it without a rider."

"I'd like to see that," Tom laughed, so of course I dismounted at once.

"Come on Jade," I said and ran back toward the poles, with her trotting eagerly behind me.

I ran between the first two, right hand turn, left hand turn, with Jade at my shoulder, then pointed to the third and said, "GO!" She immediately curved to the left and, while I ran straight along the line of poles, calling to her, she ducked obligingly between them, her timing and technique absolutely perfect.

"Clever girl," I hugged her ecstatically at the end of the line. "You are definitely the best pony in the whole world."

"Incredible!" Tom's mouth was still hanging open. "You've got to show everyone that!"

"You think?" A big part of me wanted Zak to give me that same look of stunned admiration.

"Definitely," Tom said, looking across the field where the others were grouped. "Oh, hold on, it looks like they've got trouble."

I could hear raised voices now, and as I hopped back into my saddle I saw Ed lift his hands despairingly skywards. He turned and started walking away but Tasha chased after him, grabbing his arm and shouting. I couldn't hear what she was saying but it was obvious the infamous temper had flared and Zak's girlfriend was kicking up dirt in a big, big way!

CHAPTER FIVE

I was a little surprised that Tom didn't go charging off across the field to see what was going on.

"I'm not a fan of of fighting," he looked at me apologetically. "So I'd rather keep out of the way till they settle it themselves. You don't mind, do you?"

"Not me," I said fervently. "I feel the same way. Millie looks as though she's in the middle of it, though."

I could see her standing next to Zak, and as I watched he handed her Jet's reins and walked over to Tasha, who was now stamping her way back from the gate.

"I bet that's the end of this morning's session," Tom said. "Zak will go running after Tasha now, so we might as well walk the horses back to the yard."

"OK," I agreed. "Jade deserves a good long rest after all the hard work she's put in this morning."

"And we've got the beach ride later," Tom said, as if I *needed* reminding.

"I'm really looking forward to it and I know you're going to love it too." It was half an hour later and I was still rubbing Jade's back and chatting to her. "You enjoyed this morning but you're going to have the best time ever when you start swimming in the sea."

"Don't get your hopes up!" Millie's face appeared at the stable door. "That's what the fight was all about."

"The one between Tasha and Ed?" I looked at her. "What's that got to do with the beach?"

"Well I don't know exactly," it sounded as though Millie enjoyed a good gossip session, "but from what I heard it has something to do with having to ride over the neighbor's land."

"The neighbor –?" I shook my head. "Why would Tasha be fighting with Ed about something like that?"

"You don't know her," she said darkly. "Tasha can argue about *anything*."

"So you said," I said and kept on massaging my pony's back. "What exactly happened to set her off?"

"Well," Millie said, coming in to join me, "Ed said something to Zak about this afternoon's ride and Zak said he'd definitely need some help. There are four of you whose horses have never swum before so Zak was saying it would be safer with two instructors."

"Won't Tasha be helping him?" I asked. I was under the impression they did everything together.

"That's what Ed assumed. He threw out some remark about it and Tasha just blew up. She said to him, 'You know how I feel about the Grants; you can't possibly expect me to go.' Ed looked a little shocked and muttered something about this not being the time or the place to discuss it and then he started walking away."

"We saw Tasha run after him," I said, flexing my aching fingers. "She was really screaming by then."

"Wasn't she though? Zak tried to quiet her down but she just yelled louder."

"So what happened next?" I asked as I placed everything neatly back into my grooming kit. "Tom and I just stayed out the way."

"Ed kept on walking, completely ignoring Tasha, so she stomped back, grabbed Sabrina and took off. Zak sort of groaned and hesitated, and then he said, 'Sorry guys, let me just get this straightened out,' and he went after her."

"What did he say when he came back?" I asked, giving Jade one last pat and leaving her to enjoy her lunch.

"That's just it," Millie paused dramatically at the door. "He didn't. Come back, I mean. The four of us just hung around till Val came rushing over. She was all apologetic, and told us to bring the horses back here while they figured out something for this afternoon. Apparently she and Ed have an appointment so they can't come with us."

"Do you think that means we won't get our ride to the beach this afternoon?" I felt a sickening lurch, a double whammy of disappointment – no swim, no Zak.

Millie shrugged. "Val said they'd try, but I don't know – last year there was only Tasha helping Zak with the fun stuff like games and rides to the beach. Ooh shush – here he comes, look!"

Zak was riding into the yard, his expression hooded and somber. He slid to the ground and led Jet into his stable. I was eager to stay out of the way again, but Millie hung on to my arm so we were still in the yard when Zak reappeared.

"Hi," Millie said with artificial brightness. "Um – Caitlin was just asking about the beach ride. It's still on, isn't it?"

"Yes." For the first time he didn't switch on the fabulous smile. "We'll meet here at 3:30. Make sure you've got your swimming stuff."

"OK, thanks," we both stammered as we watched him mope away.

"Phew," Millie let out her breath in a long sigh. "Does he look angry or what! I bet you Tasha's still playing him."

"Looks like it," I agreed, thinking passionately that he deserved someone better. "But at least the beach ride's still on."

"You just can't wait, can you?" Millie laughed. "I hope it's not a massive let-down like my first experience was."

We spent the time after we'd eaten chilling out in the yard again. Corinne, Andy and Jacob were also greatly looking forward to their first swim.

"Lucas *has* actually tried before," Jacob told us. "In a river at home, but it wasn't all that deep, and I think he was just faking it."

"You mean bending his knees and pretending his hooves were off the ground?" Corinne mocked him. "As if!"

"What about you and Teddy?" Andy was very flirty with her. "Have you done anything more than wade?"

"No, but Teddy will be a natural," she said, tossing her blonde hair. "I just know it."

"I hope Jade is," I said fervently. "We've never done anything like it before."

"You hadn't done games either and you were both great at that," Tom said encouragingly. "I mean, our team beat this bunch, didn't we?"

That set everyone off in a lighthearted battle and we ended up tearing around the yard, hurling armfuls of mown grass at each other. Millie and I spent a good ten minutes afterwards picking bits of green out of Corinne's pretty hair till we all flaked out again and lay under the trees swapping funny stories about our lives and our riding. It was the first time I could remember feeling part of a group like this and I found myself relaxing and thoroughly enjoying the experience. I still wanted to see my Best Friend Forever Jade of course so, half an hour or so before we were due back in the yard, I slipped away from the others so I could spend some time with her.

She'd eaten all her lunch and was drowsily resting in the cool shelter of her stable, but she gave an immediate whicker of pleasure when I opened the door. I gave her a cuddle and told her what I'd been doing, stroking her gently so that she closed her eyes and leaned against me. Gently untangling some strands of her mane, I kept my voice low so as not to disturb the lovely serenity of the stable block, and got a big shock when a sudden, strident voice shattered the peace.

"So what you're saying is, you support your parents rather than me. Thanks for nothing, Zak!"

It was Tasha, and though I was hidden from view in a corner well back from the door and couldn't see her, I could imagine the explosive fury on her face.

"Oh come on Tasha," Zak sounded weary and very fed up. "It's not like that, you know it isn't. I'm part of the family business so I have to stand by my dad's decisions."

"Even though he's practically calling me a liar?" A door clicked shut and I realized she was in the adjoining stable with Sabrina.

"He's not calling you a liar, he's just accepting the situation as he sees it," Zak said, having followed her in.

"Yeah right. He believes Ray Grant's telling the truth and I'm not – it's the same thing."

"No it isn't. Grant has proof, Dad says, and the fact that you don't believe in it doesn't make you a liar – just mistaken, that's all."

"Mistaken!" Her voice went an octave higher. "I'm not mistaken about the way he cheated my uncle over a property deal last year, am I? You knew about that and yet you're on your parents' side, not mine."

"It's not a question of sides," Zak said, obviously losing patience. "The coast ride is an important part of the vacations we offer. I can't go shooting my mouth off at the neighbors when I've got nothing to support what you're saying."

"So we're back to square one. You'd rather stick with your family and your business than me, even though if I'm right –"

"You see," he interrupted harshly. "You're saying '*if*'. Admit that you're not one hundred percent sure about this, Tasha. You just don't like Ray Grant and you're using this obsession to try and start some sort of feud."

"It's not an obsession! My uncle's got first hand knowledge of his dishonesty and that makes me suspicious of the way Grant *conveniently* discovered his so-called evidence. You and your family are far too trusting – oh, we're never going to agree about this so maybe I'd better just go, Zak."

"You can't go," he said flatly. "You're booked to take the beach ride with me. You were happy enough to take this summer job when my parents offered it to you, so you *have* to honor it."

"That was different," she flared again. "It was before –"

59

"Before you started fighting with Ray Grant," his voice became fainter as he moved away, "You're always fighting with *someone*, Tasha. Just get over it!"

As his footsteps faded I distinctly heard Tasha start to cry and wondered briefly whether I should say something. My dislike of any sort of emotional confrontation made me stay quiet and I was very relieved when, after several loud sniffs, she too walked out of the stable, closing and bolting the door behind her. After a few minutes I risked peeking out and was very happy to see an empty, quiet yard once more. It would soon be time for the others to arrive and start getting their horses ready for the afternoon ride – if, after what I'd just overheard, it was actually going to happen. I fetched Jade's tack and grooming kit and returned to her stable just as Tom appeared.

"I wondered where you'd gone," he said, grinning at me cheerfully. "I should have guessed you were here!"

"Mm," I answered, I wished I knew him well enough to confide that I'd been unintentionally eavesdropping. "I was just keeping Jade company for a while."

"Have you been discussing tactics for your swim?" he teased, holding the door open for me.

"Nah. Everyone says she'll either love it right away or –"

"Or she won't," Millie had arrived. "I'm just hoping Chas will remember how much he loved it last year. It took a while but we got there eventually, didn't we Zak?"

"That's right," answered Zak. He had just walked in. The brilliance was gone from his blue eyes and it was an obvious effort to smile. "Is everyone here?"

I found I was digging my fingernails into the palm of my hand, willing him not to say the ride was canceled.

"Yeah, here we are," Corinne said as she, Andy and Jacob rushed over to get their saddles. I relaxed and tried to feel more hopeful.

There was no sound coming from the stable next to mine and it wasn't until I was tightening Jade's girth that I heard Tasha go in and speak quietly to her pony. I led Jade into the yard and, what with feeling slightly apprehensive about the ride and *very* nervous about Tasha's temper, I was more subdued than usual.

"Don't worry, Caitlin," Millie said, assuming I just had a bad case of riding nerves. "You'll be fine even if you fall off. It doesn't hurt – you just get a little wet, that's all."

"I haven't fallen off in years," Corinne said, tucking her hair carefully under her helmet. "And neither has Andy. We were just talking about it."

"I fall off a *lot*," Jacob said ruefully. "So I'm expecting to get pretty soaked."

"Hopefully not," Zak said, already mounted on Jet. "But if any of you do fall off can you please try to hold on to your horse's reins? It'll be hard for me to keep an eye on everyone if I'm chasing after loose ponies the whole time."

"You talk as though you're taking this ride out on your own," Tasha led out the pretty palomino Sabrina.

"I – um –" The look Zak gave her was an almost comic mixture of relief, gratitude and exasperation. "No, of course not. Tasha will be there to help too, of course."

"Of course," she repeated, swinging easily into the saddle. "It's my job; it's what I'm paid for."

I saw Tom blink, but no one else, not even Millie, seemed to notice the tension between the two, so I crossed

61

my fingers superstitiously and hoped that everything was going to be all right. We rode out in a double line, with Zak and me leading, followed by Corinne and Andy, then Tom and Millie, with an ecstatic-looking Jacob bringing up the rear with Tasha. At first we followed the trail we'd taken the day before but when it divided into two we took the right hand fork, cantering along a broad swathe of grass bordered by a row of heavy-duty fencing. Zak, still deep in thought and uncommunicative, checked the route ahead and held up a hand to show that we were slowing down. A young man, loading wooden posts onto a pickup truck, waved a greeting.

"Off to the cove?" he asked, his thin face very tanned.

"Uh huh," Zak nodded. "We've got four new guests in this group and they're all eager to swim."

"Is that right? Make sure you warn them to stay away from Tyber cliffs. There was another fall last week."

"Will do, thanks. See you later," he answered. As he led us away, Zak gave me the first proper smile of the afternoon so I felt encouraged enough to speak.

"Why did the man say that?"

"Paul? Oh, about the cliff you mean?"

"Yes. Has someone fallen into the sea from where you showed us yesterday?"

He laughed, his face relaxing finally into its more natural good-looking lines. "No, don't worry, Caitlin. Paul's an avid fisherman, always out in his boat, and he was warning me about rock falls. It's nothing serious, but it makes sense for us to keep away from that part of the bay."

"Oh, OK," I said, relieved. "Where are we going now?"

Keeping to the line of the high fence, Zak was leading us toward a heavy metal gate.

"Our route takes us across the edge of a neighbor's land," he said, not looking at me. "He's very kindly allowing us to ride through his property. I'll open the gate so you can ride in, then just wait till I rejoin you. OK?"

"OK," I kept my voice and my expression non-committal.

We were obviously about to enter the grounds belonging to Ray Grant, the neighbor about whom Tasha and Ed had quarreled so violently. I did exactly as Zak said, walking sedately through the open gate, then bringing Jade to a decorous halt a few yards on the other side. I was itching to turn around and see how Tasha was reacting but thought I'd let Millie tell me later – she was bound to be watching for any possible fireworks! Zak still seemed tense as we rode quietly along the tree-lined trail. There was no sign of a house, so I imagined it must be further over to our right, but as we moved forward the salty tang of the air became more pronounced and soon I could hear the wonderful sound of the sea. We emerged from the trees onto a stretch of scrubby looking grass which quickly gave way to dark, coarse sand, graduating into the fine, pale gleam of beach we'd seen the day before. Once again I drew in my breath as I took in the view – the sweeping curve of the bay, encircled by towering cliffs of slate gray, the gentle waves lapping on the shore while ocean breakers threw up clouds of white spray further out among some rocks. And the sea itself, an endless, rhythmic mass of deep blue, shading into azure, cobalt and turquoise. I exhaled at last, feeling Jade twitch and prance beneath me, filled with the same excitement and wonder.

"Like it?" Zak's gorgeous eyes smiled into mine.

"It's – it's –" I couldn't speak.

"Come and get a closer look," he said, twisting in his saddle to check that everyone was OK. "We'll start off along the beach to give your horses a nice gradual introduction. Let them take their time to look; it's a whole new experience, so it might take them a while to settle down when we get closer to the water."

We flowed gradually into a gentle canter and I could hear the ponies behind me snorting and plunging in their excitement. Even my usually well-mannered Jade was hard to hold, bursting with enthusiasm at the glorious new sensation of sand beneath her hooves and sea air in her nostrils. When we reached the slightly damp, firmer ground at the ocean's edge she was desperate to gallop. I could feel her energy fizzing all around me and I had to hang on tight to keep her under control.

Zak grinned his approval at me then yelled, "OK, let's give them a nice gallop – just a short one, everyone."

We took off like a bunch of racehorses, plunging from canter into the exhilarating four beat time, and I laughed with sheer joy as Jade stretched every muscle in an effort to keep up with the awesome speed of Zak's Thoroughbred. She nearly made it, her pretty bay head getting closer and closer to Jet's gleaming black shoulder until Zak raised his hand again, curving his horse in a smooth arc before we reached the towering cliffs ahead. The action took us back along the sweep of the bay and meant we'd ridden toward the shore line so were now cantering powerfully through the edge of the sea itself, our horses' hooves kicking up spray which cascaded in a million shining drops around us. We dropped the pace further and, well before we neared the rocky outcrop at the other end of the bay, our horses were walking, splashing their way through the crystal clear waves beneath them.

"Give Jade a long rein so she can investigate," Zak shouted, smiling at my overjoyed expression. "But be careful she doesn't decide to roll. That's caught plenty of riders by surprise before."

I watched my pony's intelligent eyes take in the vista, laughing as she reached down and blew curiously at the strange, salty element swirling around her feet.

"Ooh!" Corinne shrieked. "Teddy's pawing at the water – is he going to lie down?"

"Keep him moving if you think he might," Tasha said, still unsmiling, and rode close to her. "How are the rest of you doing?"

"Great," Millie said, grinning from ear to ear. "I think Chas is going to be all right, Zak."

"Good," he said, moving Jet further into the waves. "We'll take their saddles off soon so you can try him out further in."

Tom, on the super-cool Fenton, was also wading knee deep and I asked Jade to follow, not sure what she'd make of it. She joined him at once, seeming to revel in the feel of the cool water around her legs.

"Hey, not too deep, Caitlin," Zak called out. "You nearly got wet boots just then."

All the horses seemed to be enjoying their first experience with the ocean so after a while Zak said we could un-tack and get ready to go in a little deeper. I literally couldn't wait and, having whipped off Jade's saddle plus my boots and breeches, vaulted onto her bare back before anyone else had finished stowing their gear on some dry rocks further up the beach.

"Wait for me," Tom called, hopping effortlessly onto Fenton. "You've still got your T shirt on anyway."

Being pretty shy, I'd deliberately worn a baggy number that covered my swimsuit.

"I don't think I'll get it wet," I said quickly. "Jade probably won't want to go in that deep, so it won't matter unless I fall in."

"*That* is always a possibility," Millie said, clambering back on Chas. "And if I had a figure like yours I wouldn't cover it up anyway."

I poked my tongue out at her and glanced quickly around, wondering if Zak had heard. Stripped to a pair of shorts, he was one heck of a gorgeous sight but his whole attention was focused on Tasha who, still pouting and sulky, was a total knockout in a cute bikini. Zak's eyes said it all; despite the aggravation she was causing him he was still utterly besotted. Still, I told myself irritably, now was not the time for me to get an attack of jealousy – now was the first time ever I was going to swim in the sea with Jade. Taking a deep breath, I moved her forward – we were on our way to the shining, moving mass of ocean!

CHAPTER SIX

Tom rode beside me, both he and his horse seeming very laid back and cool about the whole thing. I, on the other hand, was practically shaking with anticipation and Jade was prancing and snorting excitedly.

"Calm down, you two," Tom grinned at me. "You're like a rocket about to explode."

I breathed deeply and tried to relax as we walked into the shallow edge of the sea. Here, on the shoreline, it lapped gently, almost lazily, each wave outlined with a fine, lacy foam. With every step I could feel its power increase, swirling strongly around my pony's legs as she and Fenton moved into deeper water. The sea now reached her shoulder and I loved the feel of cool, silky water on my bare feet and legs. We'd reached the coastal shelf, the point where many horses refuse to go any further, but I knew my own wonderful pony. She and I felt completely attuned, moving through this glorious new element as if we'd been born to it.

And then, suddenly, "You're swimming!" Tom said.

I couldn't reply; the amazing sensation as Jade moved powerfully, easily through the deep blue of the ocean completely took my breath away. It was like being astride a dolphin, with every muscle in her wet, shining body rippling beneath me. The waves, stronger out here, swelled around us and she breasted them joyfully, swimming into each one with effortless ease.

"Wow, she's good!" After a while Tom was struggling to keep up with us. "I thought Fenton was at home in the water but your horse must be part fish!"

"Jade's a sea horse," I called back dreamily. "It feels as though she could do this forever."

"Yeah, well I hate to spoil the mood, but you'd better not. We can't go any further or any deeper. Can't you hear Zak yelling?"

"Oh?" I shook my head in an effort to return to reality.

Zak was indeed yelling so I obediently turned my pony, reveling in the way she responded, and began swimming back the way we'd come. I hadn't realized just how far we'd traveled. The others seemed a good distance away with three horses swimming fairly close to the shoreline while the other three were still in the shallows.

"Millie and Chas are doing OK," Tom pointed to the girl's dark head.

Chas was very close to Zak's horse, looking like a wet, bright chestnut against the sleek brilliant black of Jet. Lucas was swimming too, his chunky piebald body cutting beautifully through the water while a delighted Jacob whooped with glee.

"He can do it! My horse can swim!"

"He's great," I called back, waving madly.

We'd nearly reached the trio and Zak said huffily, "Well thanks for joining us, you two! I thought you were heading for the open sea the way you were going!"

"Sorry," I said, bringing Jade alongside. "Tom had to remind me about not going out of the bay or too near Tyber Cliffs."

"Didn't you realize how far you'd gone?" Millie

asked, slithering around on her horse's wet back. "I've never seen a horse go so fast in water."

"Jade's a natural," I said proudly and Zak gave me a reluctant, but still gorgeous, smile.

"She sure is, but don't go nuts. This is a safe, sheltered bay but it's a different story beyond those cliffs."

"OK, I'll be careful," I promised. I was actually feeling wild and reckless for once, but I knew he was right. "How are Corinne and Andy doing?"

"Not too well," Millie tried not to giggle. "Darling Teddy won't go in any deeper than his knees and Blaze is pretty spooked too."

As we watched, Tasha tried leading Corinne's pony forward, getting Sabrina to walk confidently into the deeper water. The bay Teddy took two steps then stopped dead, nearly dragging Tasha off her horse's back. Tasha patiently turned the palomino and went back, this time getting close behind Teddy and trying to push him.

"Leave him for now," Zak called out to her. "Corinne, just get him to relax and enjoy wading while Tasha tries Blaze again."

"I can't understand why he's being so naughty," Corinne yelled back. "He usually does everything I ask."

"Don't worry, some horses need to take their time. Try leading Andy in, OK, Tasha?"

His girlfriend gave him a withering look and silently took hold of Blaze's reins. With a lot of positive riding and encouragement the chestnut horse slowly moved forward. At the point where the seabed shelved into deep water he threw on the brakes briefly, but Sabrina kept going and Andy stayed calm but firm until Blaze suddenly gave in, joining the palomino to swim through the gentle swell of the waves.

"Great. Well done, Andy," Zak turned Jet toward Tasha. "And – um – thanks, honey."

"Oh I'm honey now, am I?" She almost spat out the words and I saw Zak's shoulders sag.

We all pretended we hadn't heard, but I saw the way Millie looked and knew she was feeling the same sympathy for Zak and dislike for Tasha that I was.

"Try swimming alongside Jade for a change," Tom said to me, and he lightened the mood by sliding off Fenton's back into the water. "It's a lot of fun."

My T-shirt was already soaked so I joined him, kicking my legs hard to keep up with my horse.

"She's too fast for me," I sputtered. Within minutes I was gasping. "I'm just being towed along."

"If I get off I'll never get back on!" Millie shrieked but she flopped into the sea anyway.

Jacob was the best in the water, doing an effortless backstroke while Lucas swam happily beside him.

"Come on, Corinne," Zak said. He had given up trying to placate his girlfriend. "Try again. Teddy might be more interested now that all his friends are out here."

Corinne did everything she could and actually managed to get her horse almost chest deep.

"You're practically there!" Zak was all encouragement. "One more push!"

I heard Tasha mutter something irritable as she turned Sabrina toward the shore. "I'll give you another lead, Corinne," she called impatiently. "Get ready."

"I don't think –" Zak began, but again she flashed him a look that would freeze a hotdog so he shut up.

71

Sabrina, swimming strongly, approached Teddy, and Tasha leaned over and grabbed a rein. "Now push! Go on, lots of leg!"

Poor Corinne did her best and for a while it looked as though they'd won, with the bay horse nearly making the deeper water, but at the last moment he stopped dead and jerked his head defiantly back. Tasha didn't stand a chance, having been surging forward one handed on the slippery wet back of her pony, and she was yanked through the air to fall with a resounding splash directly in front of Teddy. He reacted by half rearing in the water, dumping Corinne practically on top of the other girl, then spinning around to wade back into the shallows and up onto the beach.

Zak was amazingly quick to react, riding Jet after the fleeing horse immediately. The rest of us watched open-mouthed as Tasha, her gorgeous red hair plastered like a strand of old wet rope down her back, swam after her own horse. I managed to move Jade quickly enough to block the palomino's route and leaned over to catch her reins and bring her alongside. Tasha swam toward us and clambered silently onto Sabrina's back. She always wore makeup, I'd noticed, but now it had run and was streaked down her face, and her eyelashes, without mascara, looked stubby and pale.

"Thank you," she said stiffly and I had to try really hard not to smirk.

Corinne, her own carefully coiffed hair hanging like rats' tails around her face, was plodding back to shore.

"No one's hurt, that's the important thing," Millie said in a high, artificially bright voice, and I knew she was trying not to laugh.

Zak had caught Teddy and was leading him back from the sea's edge toward Corinne.

"I think we'd better join them," Tom muttered.

Andy, who'd only had a short swim, was already pointing Blaze shoreward, and as soon as he reached it he jumped down to comfort Corinne. She was remarkably philosophical about the incident, thanking Zak for rescuing Teddy and even apologizing for letting him go.

"The reins just slipped out of my hands. Well actually, Tasha pulled them, so I couldn't hang on to him like you said."

"Don't worry," Zak said. He still hadn't risked looking at his girlfriend. "Your horse will definitely go in another day – he just isn't ready yet."

While we were all toweling ourselves and our horses down, Zak and Tasha moved further along the beach where it was obvious another fight was taking place.

"She's giving him a hard time because *she* was stupid enough to get soaked," Millie said indignantly. "It was her own fault!"

"Yeah maybe," I said, thinking strongly that Tasha should stop sulking, stop fighting and start being supportive of her fabulous boyfriend but I was still trying to keep my feelings for him hidden. "She was pretty upset before we even got here so we shouldn't be too hard on her."

Millie made a rude remark which everyone heard, but it sounded so funny coming from her that we all burst out laughing.

"Glad to hear everyone's still happy," Zak came over to join us.

He looked far from happy himself, the tense, worried

expression etched even more deeply on his handsome face.

The sun was very warm in this lovely sheltered cove and, combined with a gentle sea breeze, soon dried the horses as we lazed on the beach. Corinne was able to stuff her uncharacteristically messy hair under her riding cap and we all saddled up for the ride back. Tasha had cleared the streaks of makeup from her face but was looking tired and depressed. The magnificent cascade of her hair was still damp, staining her shirt with seawater, and she remained silent and aloof from the rest of us. Zak led the way across the beach onto the grass, this time accompanied by a very animated and talkative Millie. Jacob, after several attempts at conversation with Tasha, rode Lucas next to Tom and me.

"Tasha's having a major sulk," he said in a stage whisper. "And I think she'd rather be left alone."

The broad trail was easily wide enough to ride together, and even when we saw a tall figure striding toward us we didn't have to split up.

"Afternoon, Zak," the man called, nodding curtly. "All of these people are your guests, I take it?"

"Yes Mr. Grant," Zak looked uneasy. "And – uh – Tasha of course."

Ray Grant's eyes swiveled in her direction. "Ah yes. And she's been swimming, I see."

There was a sudden movement from the girl behind us as, apparently galvanized into action, she rode past us.

"Yes Ray, I've been swimming. Do I have to pay extra for that? I mean, surely you must own all the water in the sea here as well as all the land surrounding it." Before anyone else could speak she kicked Sabrina into canter.

"Send me the bill, why don't you?" Her voice floated back and I saw Zak's head slump forward.

"That was entirely uncalled for," Ray Grant looked extremely annoyed.

"I'm very sorry," Zak mumbled. "She's upset, and I'm sure she didn't mean it."

"And I'm sure she did. Have your father give me a call, would you?" He turned sharply on his heel and left us.

Zak closed his eyes briefly then repeated dully, "I'm very sorry, you guys. We shouldn't be bothering you with all this."

We muttered halfhearted things like, "don't worry," and "it doesn't matter," and moved on along the trail, the easygoing atmosphere replaced by an uneasy tension.

Once outside the Grant grounds, Zak carefully secured the gate. "We usually take a longer route back to Beacon Lodge from here but I'd better go straight there today to – um –"

"That's fine," Tom, seeing his embarrassment, broke in kindly. "We can always ride around your cross country course if we want extra."

"I think Jade's probably had all the exercise she needs," I backed him up. "She was swimming for a long time."

"Blaze hasn't done much," Andy began doubtfully, but I nudged him hard and he tactfully subsided.

Zak went straight to the house while we got the hose out and washed the salt off the ponies. Corinne wanted to rush immediately to the shower to fix her ruined hair so the rest of us gave all the horses, including Teddy and Jet, a thorough rinsing.

"What about Sabrina?" I asked, looking into the empty stable. "Has Tasha put her right into the field d'you think?"

"She's probably taken her home." Tom gently sprayed Fenton's belly. "Her house is only about a mile away."

"Oh? I thought Sabrina lived here all the time," I said, scraping excess water from Jade's coat.

"Yeah she does when things are …" he hesitated, "… normal."

"I don't know her as well as you," Jacob said, "but I'd guess nothing much stays 'normal' for long while Tasha's around."

"She's pretty easy to rile up," Tom agreed. "But last summer it was usually fairly minor and soon over and done with. This year's different – she seems really wound up."

I thought he was being very charitable. As far as I was concerned Tasha's behavior was terrible, and the sooner Zak realized it and dumped her the better. I was still keeping a tight hold on my feelings though and kept quiet, just concentrating on getting every last bit of irritating salt off Jade's skin.

"Don't they all look gorgeous?" I asked, standing back and admiring our handiwork. "We ought to take photos, because the minute we turn them out they'll roll and cover themselves in dirt and grass."

"I thought I'd leave Fenton in his box," Tom said. "And maybe take him across the cliffs in a couple of hours to watch the sunset."

"Sounds nice," I smiled at him. "I don't suppose you'd like some company?"

"You bet." He quickly made up a couple of nets for

our ponies and we left them pulling contentedly at the hay while we took the other horses to the field.

Jet hardly got inside the gate before rolling, choosing a bare, dusty patch to squirm blissfully in. His gleaming coat was covered in a powdering of brown earth, and bits of grass stuck out comically in his mane and tail.

"I hope Zak doesn't want to ride later as well," Tom was laughing. "He's going to have to do some serious brushing if he does!"

"He didn't mention going out, did he?" I kept my voice casual. "I mean, he's not joining us on the sunset ride is he?"

"I don't think so," Tom shot me a quizzical look. "You're just stuck with me, I'm afraid."

"Great," I said quickly. "It'll be nice and peaceful, just the way I like it."

"You're not into all this drama, are you? Heated arguments and people flouncing off?"

"Not my scene at all," I hesitated. "But it certainly is Tasha's, isn't it?"

"She's got a fiery temper. Millie and I have seen her blow her top before but it was always over in a flash. She seems – I don't know – really unhappy this year, genuinely upset I think."

I privately thought she was a spoiled brat who just wanted everything her own way but I didn't say so. "Hm, maybe. I bet Zak will bring her around, and smooth over this fight between her and Ray Grant."

"That gate and the fencing around the grounds are all new," he surprised me by saying. "And judging by what Tasha said earlier she's not happy about it."

"That stuff's a bore," I said, making a face, "but I

77

wish they'd get it straightened out and stop spoiling our riding with it."

"Caitlin!" Millie shouted, thundering toward us. "Thanks for putting Chas out for me."

"No problem," I answered, looking at her curiously. "Where did you rush off to so suddenly?"

"I saw Zak coming out of the house so I thought I'd go and casually bump into him."

"Very casual," I said dryly. "What did his parents say about Tasha's latest?"

"He was pretty cagey about it, but I got the impression his girlfriend isn't too popular with either of them at the moment," she said, practically rubbing her hands together with glee. "I bet Zak will dump her if she starts any more fights."

"Even if he does it won't mean you stand a chance," Tom pointed out, a bit cruelly I thought. "You're much too young for him to begin with."

"Age should not be a barrier," she said with mock dignity. "But seriously, I know I don't have a chance or anything, but it would be a good thing if he got rid of Tasha. She just messes everything up. He'd be better off without her."

"You think?" Tom said solemnly.

"Yeah I do, and now that she's started fighting with the Grants she's nothing but a liability."

"I'm surprised you haven't managed to get the whole story on that," I told her. "Not that I'm interested – Hey, we're going for a ride on the cliffs later – d'you want to come?"

"Is Zak going?" she asked immediately.

"No," Tom replied.

"I won't bother then. Tell you what, I'll spend the time finding out all about the Grants."

"Oh goody," I pretended to yawn. "I can't wait."

As it turned out I was glad Millie had decided against joining us. The ride to the cliff top was fabulous and the well matched Fenton and Jade seemed to enjoy it as much as we did. They were fresh and eager to go after their rest and the uphill gallop to the summit was fantastic, the early evening air soft and cool against our skin as we raced shoulder to shoulder along the trail. I gasped again when we crested the top and could see the awesome sight of the ocean spreading into the distance. The sun was low in the sky, a ball of fiery red outlined in gold throwing long fingers of color across the darkening sea. In the West a lone sail showed, looking almost black against the brilliant background of sea and sky as it made its way to shore below Tyber Cliffs. We stayed well away from the edge, not wanting a repeat of Jade's skittishness, but in fact her behavior was impeccable.

"This vacation is already doing her good," I told Tom. "She's loved everything we've done and it's making her settled and happier."

"You must have been right when you told me she was a natural sea horse," he said, quite seriously. "Since she's being so good, should we risk a cliff top canter? We only walked last time up here and –"

"Gotcha! Last one to that tree over there is a – a loser." I touched Jade's sides and she took off immediately, leaving Tom and Fenton standing.

"You witch!" he shouted, and he was after me in a flash, laughing out loud as he urged the gray horse forward to catch us.

Shrieking and giggling, I swerved around in front of them as we pounded across the cliff top that was now bathed in a deep red glow. I was enjoying our ride so much I wasn't looking ahead properly, so when a tall figure suddenly appeared in silhouette against the fading light of the setting sun, directly in our path, it seemed there was no way to avoid a head-on collision!

CHAPTER SEVEN

Luckily, with a bit of neat swerving on our part, both Tom and I managed to avert disaster. I was the first to stop, bringing Jade to a slithering halt on the downward slope and turning immediately to make sure everything was OK.

"Sorry, we just didn't see you – are you all right?"

The man dusted himself off irritably. "Well, you weren't looking, were you? You shouldn't be fooling around like that up here, it's dangerous."

"We said we were sorry," Tom said as he brought Fenton back to join me. "I checked the trail first and it was clear – you seemed to appear out of nowhere."

He opened his mouth to speak and I said, "You're Paul, right?"

A wary look came into his eye. "How do you know that?"

"We met you this morning, we –"

"I got you. You were with Zak," he nodded. "Oh well, no harm done, apology accepted."

Tom, sounding annoyed, persisted. "So where did you spring up from? It wasn't from the main path. Did you climb up the cliff?"

"Yes, there's a short cut from my boat," Paul said reluctantly. "Don't you kids go trying it though, these cliffs aren't safe."

"OK, we won't," I said, wanting to smooth things over. "Thanks for your advice, and – um – I hope you enjoyed your fishing."

"No luck today," he mumbled.

"That's a shame." I was trying too hard.

"I'd better go – Oh, you can tell Ed and Val I'll be over to start work tomorrow, now that I've finished Ray Grant's fence."

"We'll tell them," Tom said, turning Fenton. "Come on, Caitlin."

"You were a little grouchy," I remarked once we were out of earshot. "What did Paul do to upset you?"

"He was quick to put the blame on us, yet we were the ones who got out of the way," Tom said, now riled up. "Saying that what we were doing was dangerous while *he* was the one clambering around on an unstable cliff!"

The rest of the ride went without a hitch and was wonderfully carefree. Cantering through the woods and grassland at the base of the inland line of the cliffs, we reached Beacon Lodge just as the last of the light was fading from the evening sky. Jade and Fenton moved happily through the gate into their field and made us laugh by taking turns rolling in exactly the same spot. They were still together when we went to fetch them the next morning.

"You two are becoming an item," said Tom, and he scratched his pony lovingly between the ears.

"That's nice," Millie, on her way to get Chas, said as she nudged me meaningfully. "It's quite a coincidence!"

"Millie's always fooling around," I put my arms around Jade's neck and breathed in her nice morning smell. "And half the time I don't know what she's talking about!"

Ed was waiting for us in the outdoor ring once we were all tacked up and ready. He looked, I thought, as though he was under a great deal of strain, but his manner was, as always, kind and courteous. We did some warm-up exercises first while he stood in the center of the ring and watched closely. There were several small jumps set up around us and some of the horses, including Jade, got very excited when they saw them. Jade loves to jump and seems naturally talented, soaring over every single obstacle and ditch that we come across when we're out with great ease and style. We haven't done much in the show jumping ring though, and the few times we tried I found she got faster and faster with each jump until we were tearing around the ring almost out of control. I listened carefully to Ed's intelligent teaching and watched the more experienced show jumpers handle the simple, inviting course he'd set out. Andy and Blaze were particularly talented and I could see the lesson held absolutely no challenge for them.

"Val has an appointment late this morning I'm afraid, but she'll happily instruct you around a cross country course before she has to go – I know that's what you want to concentrate on," Ed smiled his appreciation of Andy's excellent riding. "Corinne, you and Teddy will probably benefit from that too."

"How about me?" Millie was thrilled to have gotten Chas around the course with no faults.

"I'd like you to work on your approach a little more," Ed told her. "And the same goes for Jacob and Caitlin. Tom, you can join in Val's class if you prefer."

"I'd rather stay here and get Fenton turning more smoothly," Tom said.

"Oh, there's a surprise!" Millie made round, saucer eyes at me and I shook my head, baffled by her meaning.

I really, *really* enjoyed the lesson though, working hard at our main problem which was maintaining rhythm, something Ed informed us was essential for all successful riding. Jade took the first two jumps, placed on one of the long sides of the school, beautifully. As we turned, however, despite making sure we were on the correct leading leg in a figure eight shape to take two more jumps placed at an angle in the center, she tended to rush, making her unbalanced and spoiling our all-important rhythm.

Millie had started to develop the bad habit of dropping her head and looking down.

"Your head is the heaviest part of your body," Ed explained. "So it's a major balancing factor, and as soon as you look down your back gets round and your horse's balance is affected. Jacob, your balance is excellent but you're dropping your hands in the last stride before take-off, just at the point where Lucas needs a quiet, steady contact to give him confidence."

Part of Jade's rushing problem was caused by my trying to restrict her during our approach, over-holding her and making her tense, so there was plenty for us to work on. It was intense but Ed was a great teacher, varying the exercise and methods so that neither horses nor riders got bored. As a reward for all that concentration we took them over to the cross-country area so they could let off some steam with an exuberant canter through the woods and rolling fields. There was a huge expanse of land with two grades of the course cleverly winding through it.

"A little more practice in the ring and you'll soon be jumping the junior route," Tom told me, pointing to a solidly built wall.

"That doesn't look too bad," I said, feeling hyped. "But – oh, look at that one over there!"

An arrangement of corner rails, requiring an extremely athletic bounce jump, loomed on the rise of a slope looking, I have to say, absolutely HUGE.

"Yeah well, next year for that one maybe," Tom grinned at my horrified face. "But I can honestly see you and Jade tackling that course pretty soon."

Showing off a little, he took Fenton over the wall, cantering on easily and clearing a few straw bales stacked close behind it.

"*We* can do that," Millie announced, bouncing in her saddle. "Come on, Jacob, I'll race you."

"Nah," he said quietly. "I want to work on this problem with my hands. I hate to think I'm putting poor old Lucas off his stride."

"I feel the same way," I smiled apologetically at Millie. "Sorry, I guess you think I'm boring but I'd like to make sure I'm doing it right before I ask Jade to take this on."

"Let's just have a flat race, then," Jacob suggested. "Except I get to have a head start because my boy doesn't have your guys' natural speed."

"We'll all need a little help if we're racing Caitlin and Jade," Tom said, riding back to join us. "They're *awesome*."

"*Awesome*," mimicked Millie unkindly. "I don't believe you! 1 – 2 – 3 - GO!"

She was off like a bullet out of a gun, with Chas

scorching across the grass away from the three of us. I went after her, laughing out loud at her gall, and felt a thrill of exultation as Jade stretched into her glorious gallop rhythm. It didn't take long for us to draw level and I deliberately held Jade in line, calling out childish taunts to Millie who groaned as she urged Chas onward. We passed the chestnut horse easily, surging smoothly ahead until we were a length, then two, then three in front – and still accelerating. Thoroughly enjoying ourselves, we made a wide, sweeping arc around an enormous chair fence before slowing down and making smooth transitions down through the paces to a walk. Tom was the first to reach me, just a few lengths behind. He hadn't been able to top our speed and he now approached, laughing and shaking his fist in mock anger.

"Not fair! You left us at the start!"

"Blame Millie for that, not me," I grinned back at him. "She took off and we just followed, that's all."

The four of us walked back to the start of the course, joking and teasing one another in the easy, friendly way I was really starting to enjoy. Tom wanted to see how Val's lesson was going and Jacob decided to accompany him.

"I won't join in but it'll be good to watch and see how it should be done," he said, patting his horse kindly.

I was about to say I'd go along too, but Millie leaned over and whispered, "Come and chill out with me. I've got some hot gossip to tell you!"

We watched Tom and Jacob make their way over to the stretch of grass where Val was keeping a close eye on her two students, and then sauntered off to a quiet, shady area not far from the house.

"I'll give Jade's back a rest," I said and slid to the ground, "while you catch me up on all the latest."

"OK," she said and dismounted too. Both horses dropped their noses to investigate the grass.

I loosened Jade's girth and ran the stirrup irons up, then smoothed my hand quickly over her legs to check for heat in the joints.

"I think this is the end," Millie sighed theatrically. "Or at least the beginning of the end."

Still thinking horse, I stared at her in alarm. "Of Chas, you mean?"

"Don't be a dork. Of The Big Romance. Zak and Tasha."

"Yeah?" I tried to look noncommittal.

"Yeah. After yesterday's outburst at Ray Grant she went straight home – hasn't come back, hasn't phoned. And what's more," she paused for dramatic effect, "Zak hasn't contacted her either – he told me so."

"And that's unusual?" I ventured.

"Duh! He's always run after her like a puppy that's lost its tail. I've seen Tasha let fly tons of times; she loses her temper, rants and storms off. Zak follows, soothes her, makes her sweet again. But not this time!"

"They weren't on good terms even before we went to the beach yesterday," I said, feeling a little guilty repeating something I'd overheard accidentally, but it was obvious Millie wanted a good, girly heart to heart. "She was arguing because she thought Zak was supporting his family and the business rather than her. She said he was on their side not hers."

"What did *he* say?" Millie was agog.

"That it wasn't a question of sides, something about the coast ride being important to them and he couldn't argue with neighbors without proof. He told her she was obsessed with hating Ray Grant and was trying to start a feud."

"Phew! And yet she still went on the beach ride with us – how come?"

"Tasha wanted to take off but Zak got really harsh and told her she had to do the ride because it was part of her job. I found out she doesn't just help out on a casual basis; she does it to earn money during college vacations. Oh yeah, and then Zak said she was always fighting with someone and she ought to get over it."

"I'm surprised she didn't brain him," Millie whistled. "Well, you've practically got the whole story there, but I'll spell it out anyway. Zak only started talking to me because he feels guilty about our ride being messed up, and once he said that I sort of coaxed the rest out of him."

"At least he *meant* to tell you," I said. "It was unintentional, but I was eavesdropping when I heard, wasn't I?"

"Whatever! Don't beat yourself up about it! The whole thing hinges on the fact that Beacon Lodge is doing really well and they're planning to expand, build more rooms on the house so they can take more guests and they're going to put up more riding facilities. Like you heard though, the beach ride is a big draw for people booking here, so it was a bombshell recently when Ray Grant announced he owned the whole beach frontage in the bay and was going to fence it all. Mr. Grant had uncovered some old deeds that show the true boundary of his land and said closing it off was necessary in order to stop trespassing on his private beach."

"Including everyone at Beacon Lodge?" I frowned at the thought of losing that great cove to swim in.

"He acknowledged the effect it would have on the vacation business so after a lot of negotiating he agreed to allow access across the edge of his land, though he's charging Val and Ed an annual fee for the privilege."

"Oh, that's what Tasha meant when she yelled at Mr. Grant about paying for her swim," I remembered. "It *does* seem pretty harsh, and anyway her objection is that she doesn't believe he's telling the truth about the boundary, does she?"

"Yeah, exactly, and she's totally out of order in my opinion," Millie said. She had made her mind up. "I mean, the guy's got legal papers and everything."

"Well, Tasha obviously doesn't believe that," I said, trying to be fair. "In which case I can kind of understand her getting so mad –"

"You're the only one who can! Val and Ed are furious at the way she's stirring things up. They're afraid Ray Grant will retract his permission and include Beacon Lodge in his lock-out and that would mean no beach rides for us!"

"I wouldn't want that," I admitted. "What does Zak think? He told his girlfriend he had to agree with his parents, but what does he *really* think?"

"He thinks she should butt out; he's sick of Tasha's fighting, and I'm pretty sure he's going to dump her."

"OK. And you're pleased about that," I said, determined not to show any emotion myself.

"I'm thrilled skinny! Oh, you don't get it, Caitlin. You're so cool and detached that you don't know what it's like to feel the way I do about Zak!"

"I'll try to imagine," I said dryly.

"It's all right for you anyway. You've got a boyfriend all ready and waiting."

"Me?" I nearly fell over with shock. "Are you nuts? I don't have *any* friends at home let alone a waiting list!"

"You've got Tom. He's interested, and has been right from the start."

"No way. We're just friends, that's all."

"You only have to snap your fingers and he'd come running. Zak wouldn't do that for me even if I tattooed a sign on my head."

"He likes you a lot," I said. I wanted to cheer her up even though my own insides were bouncing around with joy at the thought of Zak being single. "He's always talking to you. Corinne was moaning about it just this morning."

"Corinne just wants to be the center of attention. Have you *seen* the way she flirts with him? Mind you, she flirts with everyone."

"Meow," I said, trying to lighten things up with some teasing. "Now you're just being catty. Corinne's all right."

"Hm," Millie said darkly. "Wait till she hears Zak and Tasha have split up. I bet she starts fluttering her eyelashes and slapping on the makeup even more."

"Poor Corinne," I said, running my hand lightly along my pony's back. "She looked like a real mess after she fell in, didn't she?"

"Like the Bride of Frankenstein!" Millie giggled. "But at least she didn't go ballistic and make a huge fuss like someone else I know."

"I'm getting bored with the subject of Tasha and her temper," I said, giving her a good-natured shove. "Change the subject, why don't you?"

"Oh all right – hey there's what's-his-name – Paul,"

she waved in the direction of the house and I saw the tall figure pause and raise a hand in response.

"Tom and I saw him last night and he said he was starting work here today." I didn't mention how we'd nearly run him over, knowing she'd probably tell her beloved Zak all about it. "I wonder what he's going to be doing."

Millie knew of course. "Clearing some land where the new extension will go. He's not a builder, Zak says, just a sort of local handy man."

"He goes fishing as well." I thought I might know something she didn't, but not a chance.

"Yeah. His boat's called *The Sea Horse*. Nice name, isn't it?"

"Are you two still yakking?" Tom called out. He and Jacob were riding toward us. "We're supposed to be improving our riding skills while we're here, not strengthening our jaw muscles!"

"Ha ha, you're such a comedian," Millie returned amiably. "Where are you going now?"

"There's a lunch time picnic on the beach," Tom said solemnly. "But we told Val you two probably wouldn't be interested in coming along."

"As if," I said, knowing he was teasing again. "Who else is going?"

"Everyone. Well, not Val because she's going somewhere, but all the guests plus Ed and Zak."

"Oh well, if Zak's going Millie definitely won't want to join us." I was getting pretty good at joining in with the banter, I thought.

"I think I'd better," she was completely straight faced. "I mean, I'll have to hang on to Fenton and Jade while their owners hold hands and gaze into each other's eyes, won't I?"

I saw an embarrassed flush creep over poor Tom's face and said quickly, "Look Jacob, Millie's hair's on fire! Better put it out, quick!"

Catching on immediately he obligingly poured the contents of his water bottle over her head, leaving her spluttering and gasping.

By the time I'd dried her off and stopped her bashing Jacob and me, Tom's color had returned to normal. As we returned to the yard, still laughing, we saw Zak, looking as though a big black cloud was directly over his head. He was obviously stewing over Tasha, I thought, and, feeling the incredible tingle the sight of him always gave me, wondered why life had to be so very, very confusing.

CHAPTER EIGHT

There wasn't much point in worrying about Zak and Tasha, so I got on with enjoying the day, which was looking really promising. We put the horses in their stables so they could rest in the shade while everyone grabbed their swimming gear and Ed and Zak filled backpacks with picnic food. Corinne, when she got back to the yard, was triumphantly waving a rubbery pink hat.

"Look what Val lent me! It's a swimming cap, so if Teddy throws me in the water again it won't ruin my hair. What do you think, Zak – cute, eh?"

He gave her a halfhearted smile and said, "I'm sure you'll look gorgeous in it."

Corinne batted her eyelashes so hard you could feel the breeze they set up, and she was treated to one of Millie's finest dirty looks.

"See what I mean," she muttered. "It's started! Zak hasn't even officially dumped Tasha yet and Corinne's already trying to muscle in."

"Put your claws away, Cat Woman," I said peaceably. "We're just going out for a nice picnic ride and swim. Don't give Zak any trouble – he looks weighed down already."

It was true; Zak seemed thoroughly miserable and I wanted to tell him he'd be fine, that he was *so* much better off without his tempestuous girlfriend.

"What are you daydreaming about?" Tom asked, stuffing towels in his backpack. "I've spoken to you twice, but you were miles away."

"Who me? Just –uh – looking forward to the beach and hoping Jade will swim like she did yesterday."

"Sure she will, but you'd better hurry up – everyone else is ready."

They'd all led their horses out and Millie was already mounted and moving purposefully toward Zak.

"I'll stay at the back with you," she said casually. "I expect Ed is leading today and – um – Chas prefers it when he's not in front."

"OK," Zak sounded disinterested but he swung into the saddle and kept Jet next to Millie's chestnut horse.

I gave an inward sigh that I wasn't going to be near him and an outward smile at Tom. "Is it all right if I ride with you?"

"Oh sure," he said, looking immediately delighted.

"Where's my dad?" Zak called across to Andy, who was nearest the gate. "Can you see him coming?"

"No," Andy peered toward the house. "Oh yeah, here he is, but –"

Ed arrived, rushing and breathless. "Sorry, I'm very sorry about this, but Val just called and I have to take something into town for her right away."

"What about the beach?" Zak looked surly. "There should be two of us with the guests –"

"Oh, don't cancel the ride please!" Jacob spoke for all of us. "We're really looking forward to it."

"You can manage." Ed looked impatiently at his son. "You lead. This group is sensible enough to stay behind you and keep out of trouble."

"Great," Corinne said, smiling sweetly. "I'll ride next to you then, Zak, since Millie's horse likes to be at the back."

He shrugged and started moving away, not bothering to speak to his father, who turned and ran back to the house.

"Wonder what's so important?" I raised my eyebrows.

"Who cares?" Millie said gloomily. "All I know is it means that flirty girl's taken my place now!"

"Don't worry," I couldn't help laughing at her disgruntled expression. "Zak's not in the best mood anyway. You can keep Tom and me company, as long as you don't make any more cracks about him liking me."

She and Chas came over with me to join Tom, and the three horses moved on amicably together. Jacob and Andy were ahead of us while Corinne, chatting vivaciously, rode Teddy as close as she could to Zak and Jet. We stayed like that until we reached the gate in the long line of the Grants' fence.

"We'll stay in single file and keep fairly quiet through here if you don't mind," Zak's face was creased with anxiety. "I don't want to give the land owner any reason to complain today."

We obligingly did as he said, although it felt weird to be creeping silently on our way to what was supposed to be simply a few happy hours on the coast. My spirits rose immediately the minute we touched the beach, though. The cove lay before us, serene and beautiful under a clear blue sky and Jade, seeing that amazing stretch of ocean, whinnied and pranced with anticipation.

"She's ready," Mille remarked. "Oh look at Corinne, you'd think she'd glued Teddy to Zak's leg, she's so close to him."

"She's probably worrying about her horse acting up again," Tom said patiently.

"You think?" Millie made a gruesome face and I laughed, too excited about swimming again to join in with getting jealous over Zak.

We did a routine similar to the day before, riding the horses along the sand and gradually getting closer to the waves. Blaze showed little sign of reluctance this time but Teddy was worse, refusing to even get his feet wet.

"I'm going to spend a little time with Corinne, helping her build her pony's confidence," Zak told us as we peeled off clothes and saddles. "I'll be keeping an eye on the rest of you obviously, but since you only have one instructor today I want you to be extra careful. Don't go too deep or too near Tyber cliffs, don't fool around too much and if anyone falls off or lets go of their horse the rest of you try to catch him. OK?"

I couldn't wait but Millie was building up to a major sulk, annoyed that her beloved Zak would be staying close to Corinne.

"Get real," Tom was fed up with her. "And get in the water – look, Caitlin's already swimming."

"Come on, Millie!" I waved ecstatically as Jade surged powerfully through the waves.

Jacob was next to join me, followed quickly by Andy.

"Wow! Get a load of Blaze!"

His chestnut horse was already enjoying himself, despite his action being slightly choppy and his nose pointing skyward. Jade looked like some kind of mystical marine creature in comparison, her outline sleek and streamlined as she swam effortlessly in line with the shore.

"Don't go too far that way," Jacob shouted, not far behind on the strongly swimming Lucas. "There are dangerous falling rocks, remember."

"Yeah I know," I said, but I just loved the feel of silky water moving against my legs. "We'll turn in plenty of time."

We met Tom on the return trip and tried to slow our pace so he could keep up.

"You're so fast," he said, almost comically astounded. "I can just about stay in touch on dry land but in the sea Jade covers twice the distance Fenton can manage."

"Lucas is really good too," I said, grinning over at Jacob.

"Yeah, it feels great to be one of the best at something." He patted his horse's gleaming wet neck.

"Where's Millie?" I asked, squinting into the sun. "Oh there she is."

"She and Andy are staying close to the shore in case Corinne manages to get Teddy in," Tom said, getting left behind again. "At least, Andy's waiting for Corinne and –"

"And Millie's waiting for Zak," I finished his sentence for him and we both laughed.

It was totally, absolutely fabulous gliding through the ocean and I that felt Jade and I could happily stay out here forever. On shore, Corinne was still struggling. With Zak's patient help and advice she was now riding Teddy through the shallows and the bay horse seemed to be enjoying the sensation of splashing in the gently lapping waves. Tom, Jacob and I were swimming alongside our ponies and I was showing off a little by letting go of Jade and getting her to follow my every movement.

She'd been doing it on land for years and I was thrilled that, despite the excitement of tackling a completely new element, she still wanted to stay close by my side.

"Look," Tom called to me. "Corinne's nearly made it!"

I treaded water and looked shoreward just as Teddy took a hesitant step that would take him across the coastal shelf and into deep water. Corinne seemed to be doing everything right but again, at the very last minute, Teddy chickened out, slamming on the brakes and twisting back into the shallows. She did really well to stay on his wet, slippery back but, slithering sideways, she lost the grip on her reins and grabbed a handful of mane instead. Teddy took off, thundering through the surf and along the beach with Zak, ever watchful, chasing close behind.

"She did that on purpose!" Millie was outraged. "Just to get Zak's attention."

"Don't be silly," Andy growled. "She was doing her best. It's not her fault."

Millie then called Corinne a very rude word and an irritated Andy moved Blaze away from her, swimming out to join the three of us in deeper water.

Zak, meanwhile, had easily caught up with Teddy and was leading him back along the beach, deep in conversation with Corinne.

"Grr! Now she's doing her 'poor little helpless girl' act!" Millie really was in a vile temper. "Hogging all the attention – I'll fix her!"

We were too far away to stop her and watched in fascinated horror as she screamed loudly, "Oh stop it, Chas, stop it!" while waving her arms around and pretending to lose her balance. "Help! Help!"

Zak's head came up immediately as he turned away from Corinne to look out to sea. With a mighty splash Millie hit the water and Chas, thoroughly alarmed, kicked out in panic, surging away from the shore.

"We'd better catch him." Tom hauled himself onto Fenton and I did the same, sliding easily onto Jade's back and turning her to cut across Chas's path.

Jacob was fast too, but it took a while before we managed to herd the panicky chestnut till I was close enough to grab his reins and bring him alongside. Being close to the other horses quickly calmed him, and we talked to him quietly, soothing his shattered nerves.

"Where's Tom?" I asked Jacob as I squinted into the sun.

"He and Andy have gone back to the shore. There they are – oh hey, something's going on!"

The direct glare of the sun made it difficult to see but we could make out a sinister tableau on the beach. Tom was standing a little off to the side, holding Jet and Fenton, while Andy and Corinne huddled together, looking down at a figure stretched out on the sand. Kneeling beside it we could see Zak, bending and rising, his dark head lowering then turning away.

"He's giving the kiss of life, mouth-to-mouth resuscitation – oh no, that's Millie lying there!" Jacob's voice rose to a squeak.

For one stupid moment the thought flashed through my brain – ooh that Millie, what she wouldn't do to get a kiss from Zak – but then reality kicked in. This was an emergency, my friend was obviously unconscious and could well be in real danger.

"Oh no, Millie!" I nearly choked on rising tears and

had to concentrate fiercely on keeping a grip on both Jade and Chas's reins.

We surged out of the water and rushed over to the group. Just as we reached Tom, Millie gave a convulsive gasp and coughed out a stream of seawater, retching and twisting sideways, her face chalk white and ghastly. Zak sat back on his heels, his shoulders slumped with exhausted relief.

"Wh – what happened?" I knelt beside her.

She rubbed her head gingerly, her shoulders still heaving. "I got a kick from Chas when he took off. Not his fault, my fault, my fault."

"Don't blame yourself." Obviously no one had told Zak how Millie had landed in the sea, "If I'd been closer you'd have been all right. It took me so long to reach you, I thought – I thought –"

He looked so deeply upset that my heart went out to him.

"She's fine, Zak, she's absolutely fine," I gave Millie a hug. "There's a bump on her head but –"

"It shouldn't have happened. Not the accident, the fact there was no one close by to rescue her. There should always be two of us, there should always –"

"Hey," Millie said weakly. "You heard my pal here, everything's fine. I'm so stupid the occasional kick in the head can only do me good!"

He tried to smile but still looked horribly shaken.

Corinne had grabbed towels and now wrapped one very tenderly around Millie's shoulders.

"Don't be nice to me, I don't deserve it," Mille said, still shivering. "Look everyone, I meant it when I said it was my fault. I pretended to fall off, but getting a hoof in the face wasn't actually in the plan!"

"Another reason for always having someone standing by," Zak dried himself listlessly. "People *do* fool around in the water, it happens all the time and we've had umpteen soakings, but never anything as bad as this."

We spent a long time drying the horses and ourselves as the sun beat down and the sea innocently lapped and sparkled on the shore. I thoroughly toweled and checked Chas over as the color gradually returned to Millie's face, and then she announced she was now very hungry and we could all stop treating her so nicely.

"Yell at me," she told Zak. "It would make me feel better."

"I feel like yelling," he admitted gravely. "But not at you."

We then settled down to our picnic and it really seemed that everyone was now enjoying it after our fright. Everyone except Zak who, sitting a little detached from the rest of us, munched his way silently through a couple of sandwiches.

Millie, true to form, was soon cracking jokes.

"Trust me to head butt my horse's hoof on the way down," she touched the bruise gingerly.

"And trust you to be unconscious during your first kiss with Zak." I thought being facetious about the incident would help reduce its horror element. "How *was* it for you?"

"Oh don't," she moaned, hanging her head. "What a total idiot I've turned out to be!"

"*You're* all right," I gave her a gentle hug. "Like Zak says, it was just a prank that went wrong."

"I wouldn't want to be in Ed's shoes when we get back though," Tom lowered his voice. "Zak was adamant about needing someone with him and he's been proven right."

"I think it'll be Tasha who gets into trouble," Corinne said, tossing her hair. "*She's* the one who didn't turn up today."

Zak insisted we take the ride back to Beacon Lodge at a very steady pace. He rode close beside Millie, even through the "single file" stretch across Ray Grant's land, and checked how she was feeling every few minutes.

"Honestly Caitlin, it was awful," Millie confided in me as I escorted her back to the house.

"I would have thought you'd lap it up," I teased her. "Zak's undivided attention – isn't that exactly what you wanted?"

"Yeah, but not like this. I feel completely guilty, he looks worried sick and it's totally my fault."

"He's already put you straight on that, so stop giving yourself a hard time about it. Look on the bright side – he's probably so mad at Tasha he'll definitely dump her now."

"Yeah, and I even feel bad about that," she sighed again.

"Hi you two," Val said as we reached the kitchen, giving us a strained but still sweet smile. "How did the picnic go?"

"Um – there was a little accident," I said, gently smoothing Millie's hair back from her forehead to show the bruise.

"Oh dear," Val bustled into action, sitting Millie down and fetching a first aid kit. "How did that happen?"

"I was being stupid, fooling around in the water," Millie said, looking deeply embarrassed again. "I – uh – pretended to fall off and it panicked Chas, who accidentally gave me a kick."

Val's lips twitched as she dabbed stuff on the bruise. "That probably wasn't as funny as it sounds, but it's just a bump. I think you'll live."

"That's a bad choice of phrase, Mom," Zak said, his face dark with anger as he stood in the doorway. "There was nothing comical about it – Millie could have died. That's right, you heard – *she could have died!*"

CHAPTER NINE

Val gave a gasp, the color draining out of her face and Millie said quickly, "I'm all right, honestly, and it was totally my own fault anyway."

"There should have been two of us," Zak was beginning to sound like an overplayed CD. "I was too far away to reach her quickly. The kick knocked her out and she was under the water a long time. She could have –"

"Yes you said." Val pressed white lips together. "I'd better call a doctor and get you checked out properly, Millie."

"No way!" she cried. "Tell her, Caitlin, tell her I'm fine."

"She seems perfectly OK. She ate her lunch and everything," I said.

"It's not the point," Zak was still fuming. "She could –"

"What's going on?" Ed made an appearance. "I've just been to the stable yard. They're talking about an accident, Zak."

"Zak, go with your dad and tell him exactly what happened," Val took charge. "Millie, you're to come up to your room with me. I'm calling a doctor."

"No – but – I don't want –" my friend's voice faded as she was firmly ushered from the room.

"Upstairs in the office, Zak," Ed was looking grim. "Excuse us, Caitlin, while we straighten this out."

I nodded dumbly and stood in the empty kitchen for a minute before making my way back to the yard. There everything was nice and normal, everyone busy and happy, chatting and laughing as they washed seawater off the horses.

"I've done your girl," Tom said. He was just starting on Fenton. "And Jacob's hosed Chas, so – hey what's the matter?"

"Nothing," I said slowly. "Well, nothing, except I think World War III has just broken out in the house."

"You look shell shocked," he lowered his voice. "I know you don't liké fights, but don't let it get to you. Millie's accident was just that – an accident –so if the family wants to fight between themselves about it –"

"It's more than that," I swept a sponge across Fenton's back. "I think this whole 'Tasha versus Ray Grant' situation has got to them. Val was genuinely upset about Millie, though – she's sending for a doctor to check her out."

"That probably makes sense, but you don't need to worry about your little friend, you know. She's as tough as they come."

"I just want everything to be – to be *nice*," I said. "This is such a great place and it's being spoiled for everybody."

"As I said, none of it is our business so let's just enjoy our vacation and let the Meadows family sort out their own problems."

I knew he was right but I couldn't help worrying that Zak was now so mad he was on the point of quitting. As usual I seemed to have gotten things completely wrong. We were going to have some games practice later, before having another short jumping session with Ed, and to my great relief Zak was already in the field waiting for us. Keeping him company, with a grin as wide as the ocean, was Millie.

"Chas and I have been told to take the rest of the day off," she told me importantly. "No riding for me, so I volunteered to be Zak's assistant instead."

"There's a surprise! How are you feeling?" I couldn't help smiling at her obvious delight.

"Great. Fine. Oh, but," she said, lowering her voice conspiratorially, "I might occasionally feel faint if Zak forgets to pay attention to me!"

"You're shocking," I laughed and went to join the others for our warm up.

"We're not going to compete today," Zak told us. He seemed to have recovered his normal good mood. "There will be a mini show later in the week where you can test your skills, but for now I want you to start honing some of the techniques needed."

He got us doing some exercises while riding: bending to touch our toes, standing in the stirrups and stretching, and dismounting on the move.

"Stating the obvious, make sure you land facing forwards and start running the moment your feet touch the ground," Zak said. He got us riding in a wide circle while he and Millie stood in its center. "I'd like to see you do this on alternate sides. That's something your pony may not be used to, but it can prove invaluable in competition."

At one point he walked over to Corinne and adjusted the angle of her lower leg, but most of the time he stayed close to Millie and *she* never stopped smiling.

The exercises were a big help and when we also went over the vaulting technique I'd learned the day before I was pleased to see the improvement Jade and I had already made. Tom told everyone about my "loose schooling" demonstration – the way I'd taken my pony along the line of bending poles – and Zak immediately wanted to see us perform. Feeling pretty self-conscious I did it again, with Jade, bless her, co-operating beautifully.

"If I let go of Lucas's reins like that he'd just drop his head and eat," Jacob said, impressed.

"And Blaze would freak out completely." Andy couldn't believe it. "You're not even touching your pony, it's all voice control."

"That's right," I was embarrassed at being the center of attention but very proud of Jade. "If I run in and out of the poles she'll follow me, but she's also happy to do it this way too."

"It's amazing," Zak said, the most animated he'd been all day. "You two will be unbeatable once you've learned how it's all done!"

I completely enjoyed the afternoon training session and, when we moved on to the schooling ring, was thrilled to find that my show jumping was also continuing to improve. As usual I spent much longer in my pony's stall than anyone else and was still happily cuddling with her when I became aware of voices in the yard.

"So you don't want me to tell her what's going on?" It was Zak's voice.

"Tasha's so hot-headed, we'd prefer that she not know anything," Ed replied. "We feel guilty about shutting her out, but we can't risk her blurting out what we're doing. I still think Ray Grant is perfectly honest – tough and a little ruthless, but if he's legally entitled to that land then that's it as far as I'm concerned."

"But Mom's not so sure?"

"Well, she didn't believe Tasha at first. She thought she was doing her usual drama queen act, but the rumors about the guy are troubling, so she's decided to investigate his claim a little further," Ed sighed. "It's already been a long process and your mother wants it kept quiet because she doesn't want things jeopardized by one of your girlfriend's outbursts in front of the guests. They should be thinking about enjoying their vacations and taking in new training ideas – we don't want them concerned with our problems."

This put me in an awkward situation. Did I now pop my head over the door and say, "I'm still here and I heard what you said," or did I stay put and keep quiet? I chose the least confrontational option and kept very still.

"They're a nice bunch of kids," Ed continued. "And deserve better attention, but with a little juggling we'll make sure they get all the riding they want."

"Yeah, you're right. I've just got to find a way of telling Tasha the beach trips are still on."

"Absolutely, as long as she's not involved in taking them. Val says we can't risk upsetting Ray Grant again." Their voices faded as they moved away, and when I finally looked out the yard was empty.

"Honestly, you'd think wanting to spend as much time as I can with you couldn't possibly get me into trouble, but it seems to be turning me into some sort of spy!" I told Jade as I kissed her nose fondly. "Still, at least I overheard good stuff about the riding this time."

She nudged me as if in agreement and we both

stepped out of the stable for the short walk to the field. Fenton was close to the gate and greeted her ecstatically, practically ushering her across the grass to their favorite rolling spot. I watched for a while until they both settled down, and then I returned to the house, feeling contented and happy. Tom was hovering in the boot room, his face breaking into a smile as soon as I appeared.

"I was just coming to look for you, Caitlin. Everything OK?"

"Everything's great," I said and kicked my boots off. "I was just spending some time with my Very Best Friend."

"But Millie's in the – oh, you mean, Jade don't you?"

"I do," I grinned at him, glad I never felt shy or awkward in his company. "She always treats me better than the human variety."

"That's nice," he gave me a sidelong glance. "But some of us two-legged friends think you're pretty cool too, you know."

I thought it was sweet of him to say so but soon found myself in the sort of muddle I seemed to get myself into when it comes to people. Millie was almost hyper with excitement, having spent most of the afternoon as Zak's "assistant," and she'd convinced herself that there was a future for the arrangement.

"Zak's so *great*," she sighed. "And he seems totally over his sulk about Tasha. I think his parents made him realize he's better off without her."

I very nearly told her what I'd overheard. Zak hadn't sounded like someone who'd happily dumped his girlfriend – in fact he'd been planning the best way of keeping her away from the beach, but firmly in his life. The snatch of conversation I'd heard about the boring land boundary wasn't conclusive so I decided not to burst Millie's bubble and tell her I thought Tasha was still very much in the picture. She'd soon find out anyway, I figured, so why get involved?

❁ ❁ ❁ ❁ ❁

The next morning we were supposed to be having cross-country training with Val, but as we were saddling up Ed told us that some rescheduling was necessary.

"My wife has to go out on urgent business again," he apologized, "but I promise anyone who wants it will get a training session later in the day. Meanwhile you can choose between show jumping or mounted games practice, with Val offering dressage tomorrow."

"What about a beach ride?" Jacob asked. He loved the swimming as much as I did.

"Uh – yes, Zak and I will be escorting a group to the cove for anyone who'd like another picnic."

"Count us all in then," Andy said, sounding enthusiastic. "Oh sorry, Corinne, would you rather not?"

"No I *want* to get Teddy in the ocean," the blonde girl sounded determined. "He nearly made it yesterday till –"

"Till I made a total dork of myself," Millie finished cheerfully. "Don't worry, everyone. I learned my lesson and I think Chas deserves a nice peaceful swim to restore his confidence, so I'm up for it too."

"Then it's settled," Ed said, and he started spreading the sack "mats" on the ground.

"I'll do that for you," a new voice said. We hadn't heard Tasha's quiet arrival. "If you want me to, that is."

"Of course I do." Ed's smile of greeting was slightly wary but Zak's delight at seeing her shone out of every pore.

Tasha was on her best behavior, being helpful and sunny with everyone and a real asset to Zak's teaching.

"It's not fair," moaned Millie. The poor girl was sunk in gloom. "As soon as she turns on the charm Zak goes to pieces. He's looking at her like she's the best thing since plasma TV, and totally forgiven her for yesterday."

"Oh well," I said. I was pretty depressed at the gorgeous redhead's reappearance too, but didn't admit it. "It probably won't last – that temper of hers is bound to erupt sooner or later."

On that score I was proven right a lot quicker than I imagined. We had a great games session. It was hard work but really good fun, and after eight games the score was tied, with both teams winning four games each.

"What shall we do for a tie-breaker this time, Tasha?" Zak asked, looking at her lovingly.

"The bride and groom race was a hit last time," she said, smiling flirtatiously back at him, "but we could give it a new twist. This time the girls have to rescue the boys."

"Great idea," Zak said, and I saw a gleam appear in Millie's eyes at the thought of Zak seated behind her with his arms wrapped around her waist.

I knew that was what was going through her mind because I was looking forward to exactly the same thing! The guys all dismounted and hitched their horses to the fence, and just as they set off for the pick up point Ed strolled over to watch.

"Val's about to leave," he told us, "so I thought I'd come over and cheer you on, now that I've got the picnic all ready."

"Picnic?" Tasha, on Sabrina, was only a few feet from Jade and me and I clearly heard her sharp intake of breath.

"Uh – yes, didn't Zak tell you?" Ed looked at his son's retreating back. "He and I are taking the guests to the beach."

"Where? To the cove?" Tasha' voice rose higher. "Across Ray Grant's so-called land?"

"I thought you understood the situation," Ed said stiffly. "If not, I'll discuss it later."

"You'll discuss it now!" She turned on him like a flame haired tiger. "I assumed you realized I only came back on the understanding we no longer pander to Ray Grant's illegal demands."

"And I assumed you understood we still use the route but *you* are not to be involved. Val's apologized to Ray Grant for your tirade and –"

"She's done *what*?" Tasha screamed and Zak spun around and stared at them both in horror. "How can you humiliate me like this, getting Val to apologize? I – I – oh, wait till I get my hands on her!"

She spun Sabrina around and began galloping across the field.

Zak, running desperately, yelled, "Caitlin, go with her! Don't let her reach the house!"

Yeah, I know what you're thinking. Me, with my hatred of confrontation, arguments and all highly charged emotional situations, being instructed to get involved! It must have been an instinctive reaction to the passion in Zak's voice because I found myself touching Jade's sides to perform a perfect forehand turn so I could race after the rapidly disappearing palomino. Jade's great speed meant we weren't far behind, arriving outside the front door of the house just as Tasha wrenched it open. She'd leapt off Sabrina and looped her reins over the fence so I

114

dismounted rapidly, calling, "Wait for me Tasha, wait," as I followed. I could hear Tasha yelling Val's name as she ran upstairs and, although I had no idea what I was going to *do* in this explosive situation, I kept racing after her. I reached the broad landing at the top of the stairs and looked around wildly. For a few seconds I had no idea where she'd gone till I heard her shout loudly.

"Tasha!" I called, my voice slightly trembling.

She came stalking out of the door to my right, from the room used as an office by Ed and Val.

"She's not there, she already left," she sounded defeated. "I needed to ask why they're treating me like this. It's *their* fight I'm fighting!"

"Come on," I hooked my arm through hers (pretty bravely I thought) and led her back down the stairs. "Zak will here any minute."

He arrived just as we stepped outside, skidding to a halt on his black horse.

"Caitlin, thank you, you got her," he vaulted over the fence and ran toward us.

"Oh, I see," Tasha's eyes narrowed dangerously. "You sent Caitlin to keep me from getting to your mother. You're still on their side, aren't you, Zak?"

"Don't start. I've told you it's not about taking sides."

"Of course it is," she wrenched her arm free. "And the stupid thing is I'm on *your* side, you and your parents. It's because of you that I'm battling Ray Grant and his arrogant fence and his private beach!"

"I know," Zak moved warily closer. "But you're going about it the wrong way."

"The wrong – how can your way be the right one? Paying that man to ride across land that isn't his?"

"We don't have any proof of that and the business *needs* that beach ride."

"I should go," I interjected timidly. "Let you – um – sort this out yourselves."

"No!" To my surprise Tasha grabbed my arm and put it back through hers again. "I need you. There's another beach ride, Caitlin. I'll show it to you and then *you* can tell Ed and Val that it's fine to use that route instead of kowtowing to Ray Grant."

"You can't involve Caitlin! She's a guest!" Zak ran his hands through his hair in frustration. "We're doing our best to keep the problem private and not spoil these kids' vacation."

"Just one ride, that's all," Tasha was practically begging. "Please, Caitlin. It doesn't mean you have to get involved in any fight. I think there's a real alternative to using the cove and if, as a guest, you could just check it out –"

She sounded so passionate, so persuasive that I found myself nodding reluctantly. "I'll take a look, but I don't think my opinion's going to influence anybody."

"It will. You're the best person I could ask. You're so sensible and level-headed."

"Uh – thanks," I looked at Zak. "What do you think?"

"If you don't mind it wouldn't hurt to try," he shrugged apologetically. "And it'll give Tasha time to cool down."

I felt her twitch angrily but with an obvious effort she stayed calm. We walked over to the fence where the three horses were waiting.

"Look at that," Zak pointed. "Jade isn't even tied."

"No, I asked her to wait," I said simply and he shook his head in amazement.

Tasha, still fired up, was already climbing into Sabrina's saddle.

"Do we need to tell Ed where we're going?" I ventured.

"No," Zak looked across the field. "He's already taken the group off for jumping so let's not bother him."

And you won't risk Tasha starting another argument, I thought as we left the field and started moving along the drive.

The first part of the ride was the same as before, turning left to follow the trail through the woods but instead of following the line of new fencing around the Grants' grounds, Zak took a sharp left fork across some scrubby common land. Tasha, eager for me to approve the route, kept pointing out its benefits, and I thoroughly enjoyed the long, exciting canter along a broad trail. As we slowed the pace I became aware of a sound in the distance.

"Is that traffic I'm hearing?" I asked.

Zak nodded. "We have to cross a busy road, I'm afraid."

"It doesn't take long though," Tasha put in eagerly.

It must have been the main coastal route for cars, with several carriageways of fast moving vehicles thundering past. Luckily Jade is absolutely bomb-proof in traffic and didn't object to crossing over to the median, then waiting for a gap and crossing again.

"See!" Tasha looked across at her boyfriend. "That was fine – Caitlin had no problem with the road."

"Caitlin's pretty special," Zak had no idea his phrase made my insides vault gymnastically. "But I think a lot of our guests and their horses would have trouble with it."

She sighed theatrically. "Well if you're going to take that attitude –"

"I'm not," he said, and he didn't look at her. "Let's just finish the ride and let Caitlin make up her own mind about it."

The next part of the route was pretty dull but perfectly safe, with a long, narrow path, completely paved so we couldn't canter, ending at another road, this one lined with houses. It was quiet, with only an occasional car or truck passing us, and as the number of houses thinned I could smell a salt tang on the wind.

"The sea's just ahead," Tasha pointed, and there it was, glinting and sparkling under the mid-morning sun. This was a much bigger cove, bordered on our right by slate gray cliffs forming a promontory, but stretching for what seemed like miles to our left.

"It's beautiful," I said honestly. "But there are a lot of people around, aren't there?"

The beach, of fine golden sand, was liberally dotted with groups of vacationers sunbathing on beach chairs, resting under striped umbrellas and splashing happily in the sea. The thought of a group of seven or eight horses galloping across the beach and surging through the waves among them was ludicrous and I knew immediately that Tasha's idea just wasn't going to work.

CHAPTER TEN

Tasha tried hard to persuade me. "It's crowded at this time of day because it's easy for people to drive here, but if we set off early in the morning or maybe late evening we should be able to get a swim."

"Yeah?" I said doubtfully. "It would have to be empty for our whole group to take over the beach, wouldn't it?"

"Not necessarily," Tasha argued. "Sabrina and I have swum here when other people are around."

"When?" Zak challenged and she lowered her eyes.

"Well, not for a while."

"You came here *once* on a cloudy day when you thought it'd be quiet and you said it was a nightmare trying to avoid the tourists." Zak made her look at him and added gently, "It's not going to work, Tasha. Unless we get here at five in the morning it's always going to be crowded – that means no picnics, no freedom, no –"

"What happened to Caitlin making her own decision?" She sounded close to tears. "You're making up her mind for her."

"He's only saying what I'm thinking," I said honestly. "This beach is like a different world compared to the cove. How come they're so unalike?"

"The cove is cut off by Tyber Cliffs," Zak explained. "There's no road access, so even the locals don't bother with it much."

"And the few that do have been excluded completely by Ray Grant," Tasha said bitterly. "People could always walk or ride along the grassy trail to get there but since Ray has claimed it belongs to him he won't allow it. He's permitted Beacon Lodge access – at a price, of course – but," she said turning to Zak, "I'll bet anything he'll stop you as well when he feels like it."

"I don't know about that, but in the meantime we *have* to comply with his restrictions." Zak turned to me, his gorgeous blue eyes filled with concern. "I'm sorry, Caitlin, you don't even know what we're talking about –"

"Yes I do. Your neighbor's got papers that show he owns the whole beach front of the cove."

"Uh – yes," the blue eyes widened. "But Tasha –"

"Doesn't believe him and thinks you should refuse to pay for the privilege of riding through there."

"You're smart," Tasha nodded approvingly. "See, Zak, the kids all know the score so your family might just as well oppose Ray Grant like I do."

"I – um," Zak must have been recalling his father's instructions not to discuss the neighbors with her, especially in front of someone like me. "Look, there's no point in staying here. We might as well turn around and go home."

"So you can be in time to help Ed with the picnic at the cove?" Tasha was starting to fume again, and all the way back she kept nagging Zak, trying to persuade him to veto the ride through Ray Grant's land.

He stayed very quiet, occasionally shaking his head at her persistence, but refusing to give way.

"You're supposed to be my boyfriend!" she yelled at one point, "But you don't act like one. I can just about

121

take your parents opposing everything I say, but not you too, Zak!"

"My family isn't against you –" he began but she was whipping up a storm.

"Yes they are. They take everybody's word against mine – look how they believe Ray Grant and take no notice of what I told them about him!"

"It's not like that –" he tried again but she pushed past on Sabrina, walking her horse along Beacon Lodge's driveway, her back stiff with anger and hurt.

I heard Zak mutter something irritable under his breath before he smiled apologetically at me.

"Don't worry, I won't let this spoil your riding. My parents will sort this out, but in a quiet, civilized way."

"It's fine," I tried to reassure him, but he looked so worried. "I – oh, there's your dad."

Ed had come to meet us, but quiet and civilized was not the way I'd describe his greeting.

"You've got a nerve!" He glared at Tasha and there were practically sparks coming out of his eyes. "I've just spent half an hour trying to calm Ray Grant down after your latest crazy trick. Just what the heck is the *matter* with you?"

Tasha blinked. "With me? What am I supposed to have done?"

"Don't act innocent with me." Ed took hold of Sabrina's bridle and led her around so Tasha was now facing back toward the gate. "Just get out and don't bother coming back this time!"

"Hang on, hang on!" Zak rode swiftly toward him. "What's this all about?"

"Your girlfriend, in her hot headed way, decided

to take her fight with Ray to a new level. She's been over there and slung my sea horse through one of his windows!"

"He *saw* her do that? When?" Zak had gone pale.

"No he didn't see, but who else is crazy enough to do something like that? The thing was in its place before I came over to watch you, and then Tasha flew into one of her rages, went and grabbed it, then flung it at the Grant's house!"

"No she didn't." Zak leaned over and held Tasha's hand. "I've been with her every minute. You're wrong, Dad."

"Who then? That sea horse could only be taken by someone in the house, and who else besides Tasha would sneak it out and use it in an act of pure vandalism?"

"You always have to blame her!" Zak was losing the temper he always held so carefully in check. "Tasha's right – whatever happens you think only the worst of her. Because Ray Grant told you she was the guilty party you took his word for it when it's probably just one more lie he's invented."

"He didn't *invent* a big lump of glass with a sea horse in it," Ed's temper matched his son's. "He heard a crash and there it was, lying in a pile of shattered window on his living room floor! He knew whose it was of course, and brought it straight here to show me. There's no doubt about that, Zak, so who do you suggest stole it – one of the guests? They're the only people, apart from us, who had access to it."

"Yeah all right then, maybe it *was* one of them," Zak shouted, making Jet twitch and stamp his feet.

"Why? What possible quarrel can they have with

Ray? It's only your girlfriend who's fighting him like an alley cat."

"Maybe someone did it knowing Tasha would get the blame."

"That makes sense," Tasha said, nearly crying. "The girls want me off the scene so they can make a play for Zak, while the guys –"

"That's enough!" Ed thundered. "Don't you think you've done enough damage to our family's business without trying to implicate these nice kids? Zak, go and make sure they're all OK while I escort Tasha off my land."

"No!" Zak's chin was high. "Tasha didn't touch that stupid sea horse and she didn't smash Ray Grant's window with it. If you throw her out I go too!"

Keeping well away and trying to disappear into the background, I was, nevertheless, watching all three of them closely and I saw, *definitely* saw a guilty expression flash across Tasha's face.

She gripped her boyfriend's hand more tightly and looked directly at him. "Thank you. You don't know what that means to me, Zak."

Still fired up, the look he gave her in return was of pure devotion and I saw Ed's shoulders slump.

"You'd both better go then," he said bitterly and turned on his heel to walk away.

I watched Zak and Tasha ride back down Beacon Lodge's drive, the black horse's sides almost touching the palomino's, until both horses and their riders disappeared from view. I felt shaky and upset and, as always, wanted a soothing chat with Jade. I took her back to her stable and she listened while I untacked and brushed her, nudging me in her gentle, comforting way.

"There you are!" Tom's head appeared at the door. "What are you two talking about?"

"Just discussing this morning's events," I said and managed a smile. "Jade agrees with me – she doesn't think much of them."

"Phew, your horse is smart! She's right – it's more like a battle zone than a riding vacation! Where did you go after you chased Tasha?"

"We went for a ride," I said vaguely, not sure if I should tell him everything.

"Excellent choice for someone who doesn't like fights. Twenty minutes after you disappeared it was chaos here."

"Oh?" I gave Jade a last cuddle and stepped outside to join him. "What happened?"

"We *were* going over to the ring for some jumping," Tom said. "But Ed was really agitated; upset by the way Tasha had acted up. He asked if we minded taking a break till he'd 'sorted' things out, so everyone kind of wandered off. Millie was looking pretty shattered so I said I'd put Fenton in his box and join her back at the house. I was hoping you'd be there, but –"

"Zak and Tasha asked me to go with them to another beach to check it out," I interrupted, realizing there was no point keeping anything secret.

"Oh. Well, we hung around, not knowing where everyone was, when the doorbell rang – a big continuous blast like someone was leaning on it really hard."

"Ray Grant?" I guessed.

"Ed opened the door and the guy just burst in waving that hefty paperweight that's always on Ed's desk. You know the one – it's a sea horse inside a big –"

"Chunk of glass? I remember Zak showing it me but

I didn't pay much attention to it. It was thrown through one of Ray's windows, wasn't it?"

"That's right. Grant was going ballistic, shouting and swearing and waving the thing around. He was saying, "She threw this sea horse of yours knowing I'd recognize it right away!" Ed tried to calm the guy but you could see he was badly rattled too. He took the paperweight and said, 'But it was on my desk this morning. I used it just before I went over to see the riders'."

"Ed told us it must have been Tasha who threw it," I said slowly.

"Yeah, well that's what Ray Grant was yelling."

"It couldn't have been. She went into the house and ran upstairs to the office looking for Val, but she didn't have time to reach the Grants' house. We were with her the whole time."

"Their front door isn't far from the end of the driveway you know," Tom said. "It's only a little further down the road on the opposite side. You can reach it in five minutes."

"Tasha didn't have five minutes."

"Well maybe she gave it to someone else," he suggested.

"We didn't meet anyone. And anyway, where would she hide a big lump of glass? She had no bag and she was wearing a T-shirt and riding pants, and there was nowhere to stash anything bigger than a postage stamp."

"Oh," Tom thought about it. "That's going to disappoint Millie. She was devastated when Tasha showed up and had Zak running after her within minutes. Millie said right away it had to be Tasha because she could easily have taken the sea horse from Ed's desk, and who else would want to lob it through Ray Grant's window?"

"Tasha's got her own theory," I said, keeping my voice expressionless. "She thinks it was probably one of the guests stirring up trouble in the hope of getting rid of her."

Tom let out a long whistle. "Is that what she thinks? Wait till Millie and Corinne hear her say that!"

"They won't get the chance," I said and hung Jade's saddle and bridle in the tack room. "Ed told her to get out, but Zak was so furious he went with her."

"You're kidding!" he gaped at me.

I shook my head, trying to look unconcerned. "At least it means no more fights, I suppose."

"Yeah and not much riding either!" He opened the yard gate for me. "I told you Zak and Tasha did all the fun stuff last year, and there's no way Val and Ed will be able to do as much."

"I guess that's an end to the beach rides then." I felt utterly depressed. No more swimming, no more Zak. "Millie will go nuts."

We found Millie in the dining room.

"Hungry?" Tom greeted her. "If so, bad news I'm afraid. There are only sandwiches in the kitchen today."

"I know, I saw Ed unpacking what should have been our picnic lunch," Millie sighed gloomily. "I'm only in here because I'm keeping an eye out for Zak. I saw him going down the driveway with Tasha. My guess is Ed's thrown her out and Zak was making sure she cleared off the premises."

"Well, you're half right," I said, and quickly told her what I knew.

"No!" she yelled, holding her hands over her ears to block out what she was hearing. "Zak wouldn't go with her after what she did!"

127

"She didn't do anything," I reminded her. "We don't just have Zak's word for that – I was with her too, and there's no way she could have flung that sea horse through the Grants' window."

"Oh come on, don't be nuts!" Millie was enraged. "She must have sneaked away when you weren't looking."

"No," I shook my head firmly.

She bounced over to me and stared intently into my face. "You're not a hundred percent sure are you, Caitlin? I can see there's just a little bit of doubt in your mind – oh tell me, please – it *has* to be Tasha and Zak *has* to come home."

I hesitated and this time Tom joined in. "Millie's right, there's something you're not telling us."

"It's nothing, it's just – well, I was watching Tasha's face and she looked guilty – only for a minute but it was there – she looked guilty."

"That's because she is," Millie crowed. "Go and tell Ed!"

"No." I was adamant. "I might have read her expression wrong, and what I saw isn't evidence, it's just an impression I got."

"Caitlin's right," Tom said, thinking hard. "So the best thing we can do is try a little detective work – find out just who *did* have the opportunity."

"More or less everyone," Millie said instantly.

"But hang on," I said as something occurred to me. "How would any of the guests know about the paperweight? Why didn't they just throw a stone or something through the window?"

"Ed showed us all his beloved sea horse, didn't he Tom?" Millie answered at once. "It wasn't long before you and Jade arrived, Caitlin. We were talking about swimming

128

and Corinne babbled on and on about how good Teddy was going to be. She said something about wanting him to be a sea horse and Ed immediately went upstairs and brought the paperweight down to show us a real one. So everyone could have known it was the perfect thing to let Ray Grant realize the damage was caused by someone from here. The question is *why* would they do it?"

"To set Tasha up?" I offered. "She and Zak thought one of us might have done it, hoping that she'd get the blame."

"Why do they think that?" Millie looked from Tom to me and back again.

"Uh – " I said, too cowardly to tell her that Tasha knew about the crush most girls had on her boyfriend.

"She knows a lot of the guests would prefer it here without her," Tom said tactfully.

"Because she's a total pain?" Millie was blissfully unaware. "Yeah, that figures."

"Come on, let's get something to eat," I started walking to the kitchen. "We could put your detective thing into practice, Tom, and find out where everyone was when the sea horse was taken."

Corinne, Andy and Jacob had already started on the picnic lunch, looking, pardon the pun, fed up.

"It's not exactly what I imagined doing on this vacation," Corinne shook her sculpted curls petulantly. "Sitting around a kitchen table instead of on a beach."

"They can't help it," Jacob said, steadily plowing through a big plateful. "Ed will straighten things out. I bet he and Zak will take us to the cove later."

"Duh! I don't think so!" Millie was all drama. "Zak isn't even going to be around, and it's all Tasha's fault."

"Hey, cool it, you," I said, helping myself to some food. "We don't know that."

"We don't know much, really," Tom said, and his manner was, as always, calm and pleasant. "It's all a big mystery. We need to find out where everyone was between the time Tasha fought with Ed and rode off and – oh let's say, half an hour later."

"Why?" Andy looked curiously at the three of us. "We heard some commotion earlier – is there trouble?"

"Yeah. Someone vandalized the neighbors' house."

"The Grant place?" Corinne raised her eyebrows. "I nearly rode in there earlier."

"Is that where you went?" Andy looked at her. "I saw you go down the Beacon Lodge driveway but when I went to find you you'd disappeared."

"When Ed canceled the jumping class I decided to take a few postcards and ride to the mailbox we passed on the way here," Corinne explained. "And I thought the turn I found was a shortcut but in fact it led to the Grants' house so I turned back to the road and saw you."

"I was going to do some work in the ring," Andy told us. "But when I saw no one else was bothering I decided to follow Corinne instead."

"Do you want my alibi now?" Jacob reached for another packet of potato chips. "That's what you're doing, isn't it – collecting alibis?"

"Uh – we're just trying to sort out in our minds where everyone was," Tom looked slightly embarrassed that his 'detecting' had been uncovered. "So yeah, we are asking for alibis I guess."

"Oh, whoops," Jacob made a face. "I don't have one.

Does that mean I'm guilty of whatever horrible crime's been committed?"

"I don't think so," Tom laughed. "Actually I was on my own for fifteen minutes and so was Millie, so none of us are in the clear."

"Except me," Corinne said instantly. "I told you where I was."

"But Ray Grant's house is the scene of the crime," Millie cried. "Tell them exactly what happened, Caitlin. You'll say it all cool and precise, not like me."

I went through the story of the paperweight through the window and how Ray Grant and Ed thought it must be Tasha's work.

"Of course it was," Corinne nodded vehemently. "Who else?"

Slightly wearily I told her how I could vouch for Tasha's innocence.

"Excuse me," Val's voice cut in. "Would you mind going through that one more time, Caitlin?"

"Sure," I got up from my chair, blushing because she'd heard us discussing her family this way.

"Come up to the office, dear," she gave the sweet smile that looked more strained than ever. "I'm truly sorry to ask you but you obviously know the situation, so –"

"It's fine," I followed her up the stairs.

I'd never been in Ed's office, which was a model of neatness and order. The walls were lined with shelves, each bearing dozens of books about horses. There were prints and photographs of horses everywhere and a big, solid desk with a leather top plus two shabby but comfortable looking chairs.

"Sit down, Caitlin," Ed said. He was slumped behind the desk, his back to the window. "I'm sorry –"

"You don't have to keep apologizing," I said quickly. "I know you've got problems and if there's anything I can do to help, I will."

"Thank you," he gave me a tired, but genuine, smile. "You told me you have the gist of what's going on, so can I ask you exactly what happened when Zak sent you galloping after Tasha this morning?"

I told them both the story as succinctly as I could and when I stopped there was a brief and uneasy silence.

"So Tasha definitely didn't leave here with the paperweight?" He moved it to a central position on the desk. "Here it is, you see."

Now that I could study it properly I could see it was a quirky kind of object. An irregular, solid looking piece of amber colored glass, shaped and polished so it reflected the light streaming in through the window, it contained in its depths the perfect, charming form of a single sea horse.

"It's very nice," I said, somewhat lamely. "But Tasha couldn't have taken it. She had no pockets, or anywhere to hide it. We left right away and both Zak and I were with her till we got back here and you – you –"

"Attacked her," Ed groaned and put his head in his hands. "I'm sorry, Val. If you'd been here you'd have dealt with it so much better."

"Ray Grant upset you," she said loyally. "He assumed right away that Tasha had caused the damage and you –"

"Agreed with him. She was like a – a demon the way she flew at me earlier, and when I told her you'd apologized to Grant I thought she was going to rip your head off."

"That's why Zak told me to stop her," I said helpfully. "So she wouldn't."

"That was very brave of you," Val said. "I've seen grown men tremble when Tasha's in a rage, but it seems as far as the vandalism is concerned we've done her an injustice."

"*I* have, you mean," Ed rose to his feet. "I'll have to go to her house and apologize, persuade Zak to return and –"

"Not yet," Val said firmly and I could clearly see who made the rules here. "Let them both cool down first."

"But I can't bear Zak turning against us." Ed was so upset he hardly noticed I was there. "You know how much he means to me. I want him here."

Unexpected tears prickled behind my eyes and at the back of my throat. My own dad had turned his back on me completely, going as far as leaving the country to begin life abroad with his new family, and yet here was a father who couldn't bear a separation of only a few miles. I felt a burning hatred for Tasha, thinking about the guilty expression, which I was sure meant *she* was responsible for the gaping rift within this once united family.

CHAPTER ELEVEN

I left Val trying to cheer Ed up and walked slowly back to the kitchen, thinking hard. Tom was right, the only way to clear this up was to do some detective work but, instead of concentrating on the alibis and motives of the guests, I needed to work out just *how* Tasha had managed to stage the sea horse stunt. Millie was waiting in the hallway to find out what was happening now.

"Is Zak coming home?" she asked eagerly, and her face fell when I shook my head. "I thought Ed would rush off and get him, you know, apologize to Tasha and bring them both back here."

"I thought you didn't want the girlfriend around," I said lightly.

"I don't really, but it's not fair for Tasha to be blamed for something she didn't do." Millie was very honest. "And I'd much rather have Zak around, even with Tasha, than not see him at all."

"Come on then," Tom said, coming out to join us. "I've got a pen and some paper, so let's go back in the dining room and make some notes."

"This is you in your role of Ace Detective, right?" I grinned at him.

"Absolutely," he sat down at the table and wrote a heading in capital letters – OPPORTUNITY. "OK," he said, pausing, "we know the sea horse paperweight was definitely on Ed's desk this morning, so who had the chance to sneak up and lift it in order to sling it through Ray Grant's window? Let's start with the people who couldn't – they are Ed himself, Val, Tasha and –"

"Hold on," Millie was frowning. "You can't rule out Ed and Val. We don't know where either of them was when the window got smashed and they could have taken it at any time. We only have Ed's word it was on his desk when he left the house."

Tom and I gaped at her.

"Um – well – yeah, but surely we know Ed's telling the truth, don't we? You saw him when Grant came bursting into the house – Ed was genuinely astounded."

"And Val had an appointment in town," I put in. "Anyway – *why* would they do such a thing? They're the ones who want to keep the peace with the neighbors at all costs."

"That's true," Millie conceded. "But I just wanted to point out that it's not just the guests who had," she ran her fingers under Tom's headline, OPPORTUNITY.

"Thanks for complicating things even more," I grumbled. "I've just been with Val and Ed and they're both totally shattered by this. I, for one, completely believe Ed's version so let's take it from there. Ed says the sea horse was in its place when Tasha and I ran into the house. She didn't take it and I didn't take it – and Zak didn't even go inside. Then we rode to the beach and didn't return till after it was all over, so I can't see how it can be any of us three."

I was hoping my fellow detectives would see a flaw in my logic, a possible method that could explain how Tasha had managed to steal the sea horse and use it without either Zak or me seeing her.

"That seems irrefutable," Tom said, pretending to be all pompous. "If Zak and Tasha had supplied alibis for each other I'd be suspicious, but the fact that you were there, Caitlin, definitely proves they're both innocent."

"Yeah, you're right," Millie sighed deeply. "What a shame, I'd love it to be Tasha! Oh well, let's see whose name can definitely go on the opportunity list."

"Mine for a start," he said and wrote TOM underneath the heading. "When Ed abandoned the jumping class I went to the yard on my own, settled Fenton down, got a hay net, all the usual stuff. I bet I was on my own for about fifteen minutes – plenty of time."

"OK, so you'd better put my name next." Millie shrugged. "I came straight back to the house and read a magazine till you came in, but I don't think anyone saw me."

"And you didn't hear anything – no one going upstairs for instance?" I asked.

"Nope. I was in the kitchen at the back, and didn't notice a thing."

"Jacob said he just hung around, went for a ride, didn't see anyone," Tom said as he busily scribbled it all down. "So he's another one who had the *opportunity* of paying the Grant house a visit."

"Agreed – he isn't in the clear either. Mind you, from where I'm standing, Corinne looks like Suspect Number One, doesn't she?" Millie laughed unkindly. "*Her* alibi is that she was riding 'by accident' along Ray Grant's driveway. Duh!"

"While Andy was also nearby, apparently looking for her," I shook my head. "Don't you think if either of them *was* guilty they'd have come up with a better story?"

"It could be a double bluff," Millie said darkly.

Tom glared at her. "Don't make this any more difficult than it is! OK, we have five main suspects, any of whom *could* have taken the sea horse and used it. Now here's the million-dollar question. WHY would Millie, Corinne, Andy, Jacob or I *want* to do such a thing?"

Watching him write MOTIVE carefully on the next line I said diffidently, "The obvious reason is to implicate Tasha, I guess."

"In which case at least four of us had a motive then," Millie cheerfully ticked them off on her fingers. "Corinne and I like Zak, so we want Tasha off the scene. Andy likes Corinne so he wants Zak off the scene. Jacob likes Tasha but she ignored him so he wants revenge."

Tom and I stared at her.

"Uh – right," he said weakly. "You don't have a motive for me then?"

"Can't think of one. The person you like –"

"You're making all this up," I interrupted quickly. "It's not for real – none of you would cause criminal damage. This is sheer fantasy."

"You think?" Millie was losing interest. "It's all very well speculating, but there's no way we can get any proof is there? Ooh, hold on, though – what about fingerprints? We could dust the sea horse!"

"Yeah, but I think I forgot to pack my forensics kit," Tom said mockingly. "Anyway the thing's been handled since then, by Ray Grant for one when he brought it back here."

"So where does that leave us?" I asked. Like Millie, I badly wanted Zak around again and getting to the truth was the only way to achieve that.

Tom shrugged. "Dunno. We could keep an eye on the suspects, and maybe try breaking the alibis they've come up with."

It sounded vague and unsatisfying and I was itching to DO something, to take some kind of action.

"I bet I could do that," Millie said, more amenable to his idea. "I'll go and have a chat with Corinne, throw in a few casual trick questions, that kind of thing."

"Yeah, of course you've got Corinne down as the person most likely to lob a paperweight, haven't you?" Tom laughed, not seeming to take the situation very seriously at all.

"Yeah," Millie chuckled in return. "She's got the temperament *and* the motive – she can't stand Tasha – and had the best opportunity of anyone, being actually on the premises around the right time. I could practically snap the handcuffs on her right now."

"Stop fooling around," I said, feeling uptight. "You've already said Corinne isn't stupid."

"In which case," Millie said, ever irrepressible, "I'll go for the next most probable. And that's you I'm afraid, Tom."

"What?" He nearly fell off his chair.

"Absolutely. It was ages before you came into the house, you said so yourself. You had lots of time to grab the sea horse, ride over to the neighbors' and throw it through their window."

He put down the pen. "You're right so far but *why* would I try to get Tasha thrown out?"

"Not Tasha – her boyfriend," Millie giggled. "All you guys are jealous of Zak because he's better looking, a better rider, better –"

"You take that back!" Tom lunged at her and she ran away shrieking, with him chasing her.

I felt irritated and annoyed at their childish behavior, which clearly showed they didn't feel anywhere near as concerned as I did about the problems the Beacon Lodge family were having. As always I took myself off to talk things through with my real Best Friend. Jade was pleased to see me and listened attentively, her sensitive ears pricked forward as I stroked her neck and told her the whole story.

"I need to do something positive, something physical," I said and she nudged me agreeably. "We've missed out on our picnic, and there's not much point joining Val's cross country lesson, so maybe we should take off and do some detective work on our own."

The thought was appealing, so before everyone arrived to tack up and prepare for Val's class I got my pony ready and rode her quietly down the driveway to the main gate. I hesitated, not sure which direction to take. There was the cliff trail, but I couldn't imagine finding any clues there, or the ride to the cove but that meant going through the Grants' land.

"I'm not sure that gate will be unlocked anyway," I told Jade. "Tom said Ray was furious about his smashed window so he's probably padlocked it shut to keep out Beacon Lodge riders."

If I was to be a detective though, I figured I needed to inspect the scene of the crime, so I eventually turned my pony right, crossing the quiet road to find the turn into the front entrance of the Grant house. Tom was right, it wasn't far, and I could also understand Corinne mistaking the turn for some kind of shortcut. There were no gates and not even a house name or number so it looked like just a gravel lane curving away between overhanging trees. Once I'd ridden quietly around the first bend it was quite a surprise to see how close we were to the front of the house. There were gates, tall wrought iron ones, firmly shut and flanked on each side by a row of solid fencing. Other than ringing the bell and asking permission to enter, it seemed impossible to get any nearer and, disappointed, I moved Jade onto the grass.

"Oh well, it was a worth a try. Let's go back and rethink this –" as I spoke I noticed the shrubbery bordering the lane point was slightly flattened, the ground around it looking trodden and muddied. "Someone's been through there. Look, Jade!"

She obligingly turned her head and pushed forward, following the line of bent branches and snapped twigs. After a few steps the vegetation thinned and I could no longer find any discernable trail but kept her walking between the closely packed trees. We were following the line of fence that presumably encircled the entire Grant land and I stopped and peered ahead. There was one panel jutting out slightly, almost as though it was loose. Jade stood completely still while I leaned out of the saddle and shook it experimentally.

"It moves!" Excited, I slid to the ground and slid the panel sideways, creating a gap big enough for us to ride through.

We were still under the shelter of trees, a narrow belt that bordered the formal, manicured gardens surrounding the Grants' house, where shuttered windows gave a blank, empty look. I hoped very much it *was* empty but was too fired up not to carry on now. Keeping well into

the shadows we moved forward till we reached the back of the house with me peering intently at every window frame.

"There it is!" I squeaked, pointing to where a sheet of plywood had been fitted, obviously a temporary measure until the shattered glass could be replaced.

I debated whether to risk going closer to look for clues but decided against it – if I was seen now I could pretend I'd merely gotten lost, but if they found me snooping around the house it would take a lot more explaining. It seemed the only thing I'd proved was that *anyone* could have smashed that window and that fact wasn't any help at all! Thinking hard, I kept on riding, looking all around me for anything that might be a clue. We'd left the formal gardens behind and, from the salty tang of the air and distant murmur of lapping waves, I realized we were approaching the beach. I still intended doing a "little girl lost" act if Ray Grant spotted me, but when Jade's hooves touched the first strip of sand all my detecting ambitions were forgotten and we both became distracted by the powerful lure of the sea.

"We really ought to go back," I said reluctantly, but she pranced and whinnied eagerly, exhilarated by the tantalizing sight and smell of the beach. "OK, maybe just a quick wade."

We splashed joyfully through the shallows, sending clouds of glittering spray soaring around us.

"Do you know," I told her recklessly. "We're already so wet, we might as well go the whole way and swim!"

She plunged and snorted – Jade's equivalent of saying, 'yes – yes – YES!', so I quickly stowed her saddle with my boots and jeans on a big dry rock. There was no hesitation at all. Jade walked swiftly, purposefully through the waves until the sea bed shelved and dropped away and there we were, swimming in the cool, silky waters of the cove. It was, like always, pure bliss, and the feeling of togetherness, a total emotional unity with Jade, was the strongest I'd ever experienced. I lay along her back, not so much riding as being transported through the ocean by a fabulous sea creature. Literally carried away by the sheer heady sensation I didn't realize how far Jade's powerful swimming had taken us until I saw we were now alongside the towering height of Tyber Cliff.

"We're not supposed to be this close." I pulled myself together in an attempt to be sensible. "Come on Jade, we'd better turn back."

The swell diversified here, waves breaking and slapping against rocky outcrops or lapping gently within the sheltered pools they made, and my eye was suddenly caught by the sight of a boat almost hidden from view as it bobbed peacefully in one of these inlets.

"Look Jade," I said, pointing to its name. "*The Sea Horse*. That's what you are too – oh!"

A dark, thin face appeared briefly from behind the boat and I realized there must be a cave cut into the cliff behind it. I certainly wasn't in "detective mode" then. In the excitement of our swim I'd almost forgotten what I was supposed to be doing, but my natural curiosity was aroused. Instead of turning Jade away to swim back along the cove, I guided her through the rocks into the pool. From here I could see inside the cave and was surprised to see two figures moving boxes around in its greenish light. Jade, swimming easily, snorted as we got nearer and one of them looked up sharply.

"Hey! Who's *that*?"

"Hi Paul," I called as I recognized him at once and waved cheerfully. "It's me, Caitlin."

"She knows you!" the other person stepped back out of sight. "*Do* something, quick!"

To my utter amazement Paul lunged forward, diving into the water and quickly reaching us with a strong over-arm crawl. I didn't have time to speak or even to think before he reached up and grabbed me, yanking me off Jade's back and into the water. I still held the reins but he wrenched them out of my grasp, as with a one-armed sidestroke he swam back toward the cave, dragging me with him. It was as rapid and as horribly unexpected as that. Within minutes I was shoved and hustled into the dank cave and could only watch in horror as Jade, frightened and disorientated without me, swam swiftly out of the sheltered pool.

CHAPTER TWELVE

My reaction was based far more on fear for my pony than for myself. I let out a scream, kicked back hard against Paul's legs and tried to break free. He howled loudly and clamped a hand over my mouth.

"What are you *doing*?" the other man sounded almost as shocked as I was.

"You said I had to stop her," Paul snarled and howled again when I lashed out with my feet once more.

"I meant go over and spin her some sort of story – not *kidnap* her!" There was real fury in his voice. "What are you going to do with her now?"

"I don't know," Paul said, his hand still covering my mouth. "Let me think. If her horse gets back to shore – ow, she's biting me now!"

"And I'll do it again," I spat out. "What do you mean *if* she gets back? I need to make sure she's safe, I'll call her –"

"You keep quiet or I'll chase her out in the ocean and drown her," he shook his bitten finger vengefully.

"But –"

"Shut up, I mean it!" he sounded as though he did so I closed my mouth immediately.

"Sit there." He shoved me roughly onto a wooden crate. "And don't say a word until I figure out what to do."

The other man called him a few choice names and the two of them went into a huddle while I peered anxiously out of the cave, my heart pounding as I tried desperately to catch a glimpse of Jade. She'd be far away now, hopefully galloping up the beach and through Ray Grant's grounds. I wouldn't let myself consider the alternative, that she'd taken the wrong turn, swimming out of the cove and even now battling the waves and strong current of the open sea. She – I stopped and held my breath. I could just make out the break in the rocks, the entrance to the quiet pool where *The Sea Horse* still bobbed gently. There, her head turning anxiously as she scoured the cliffs, was my own sea horse, Jade, not swimming away at all but looking for me patiently, wonderfully. I risked a sidelong glance at the two men and, barely moving a muscle, gave the long, low whistle my pony knew so well. Paul's head shot up as he glared at me.

"What was that?"

I shook my head as if in despair, pretending to cry until he shrugged and returned to his muttered conversation. I didn't dare risk whistling again but there was no need. Jade had heard me and was swimming strongly toward the cave, already passing the moored boat in the pool. Careful to maintain my posture of slumped defeat I waited till my pony was only yards away from the cave entrance, then with one mighty leap I dived into the water, reaching her with three panicky strokes.

"Go, Jade, go!" I wasn't riding. I was just clinging on, but she obeyed instantly, striking out across the inlet to reach the gap in the outcrop of rocks. I heard an angry roar and the sound of a splash behind us and knew Paul had dived in to catch me.

"You're much faster than he is," I whispered in my brave pony's ear. "Just keep going, Jade, swim for your life!"

147

She felt more powerful than ever, carrying me swiftly across the calm waters of the pool and I knew that even a strong swimmer like Paul wouldn't be able to match her speed. It was only when a motor roared into life behind us that I felt a stab of fear. He had swum straight to *The Sea Horse*, and when I glanced nervously over my shoulder the boat was already turning in pursuit. Jade kept going, swimming through the break in the rocks and heading straight for the shore of the cove. Paul, gunning the engine to full speed, was right behind us and I tightened my grip on Jade's mane, expecting at any minute to be plucked once again from her back. He was using a different tack this time though, sweeping past us in a curving arc, and then driving *The Sea Horse* straight at us. Trying not to scream, I touched Jade's sides and turned her away, changing direction so we were now heading seawards. The nightmare seemed to last forever; four times we tried to get past the boat and four times he headed us grimly, pushing us further and further out into the deeper waters of the cove. I knew once he'd forced us beyond the sheltering arch of the cliffs that Jade would be fighting against the colder, turbulent waves of the ocean, a battle much too difficult for even a brave and magnificent horse like her.

I could feel her beginning to weaken and desperately I tried getting past the boat one more time. Just as we turned toward the beach to face *The Sea Horse,* I saw a sight that made my spirits soar. Two riders, their horses surging strongly through the waves, were heading toward us! Paul, his back to them, his senses concentrated on trying to force Jade out of the cove, didn't see them and the engine noise from *The Sea Horse* was so loud he had no warning of their approach. I could see them clearly though, and my heart banged against my ribcage as I recognized Zak and Tasha. Desperate to keep Paul from turning and spotting them, I called out to him, my voice sounding frightened and shaky even to me.

"What do you think you're going to achieve, Paul? Let us go! You can't do this!"

"Just watch me," he shouted grimly, keeping the boat steady in front of my bravely swimming pony to block any chance of our escape.

Behind him, Jet was now so close that I could see the black horse's flaring nostrils as Zak brought him alongside the boat. Terrified and exhausted as I was, I still felt my heart leap exultantly as, with one strong, muscular leap, he leaped onto *The Sea Horse's* deck. Paul spun around, but before he could move Zak was on him, his fist curled, his blue eyes gleaming. He looked – well, just *wonderful*. Trembling, I tried to smile at him, then flinched away as he raised his arm furiously at the snarling, swearing Paul. Tasha, her red hair streaming like a pennant, picked up Jet's reins with one hand and brought Sabrina close beside me.

"It's all right, Caitlin, you're safe now. Slide onto Jet and I'll lead Jade back. You're both completely exhausted."

It was true; I could barely summon the strength to slither from my rapidly weakening pony and slump against Jet's strong neck. Tasha soothed and comforted Jade, helping her gently through the water until we all reached the shallows. I almost fell from the black horse, slithering awkwardly to stand beside Jade, my legs trembling and my arms wrapped around her while her sides heaved as she took in healing gulps of air.

❀ ❀ ❀ ❀ ❀

"So, did Zak beat Paul up?" Millie's eyes sparkled at the thought. "I bet he was fantastic!"

"I didn't see. I was a little busy getting back to shore," I said dryly. "Paul had one heck of a black eye apparently, but you'll have to ask Tasha for details."

"I don't think she could have seen much either," Tom said. "From what you told us, she was more concerned with getting you and Jade back to shore."

"Yeah, she was great." I looked at them both. "So do you want the whole story or what? You didn't take the detective idea seriously, I know, but –"

"Yeah we did," Millie was indignant. "Just not quite as seriously as you, that's all. I mean, not everybody goes storming into a criminal's lair, do they? So come on, just what *were* Paul and his creepy cohort doing out there in that cave?"

"His creepy cohort is his brother, and the police have him too. They've had a nice little sideline to their fishing expeditions," I explained. "It's called smuggling. Paul was very eager to keep people away from the cove, and particularly Tyber Cliffs where they used the cave for storing stuff. There were never any falling rocks. He made that up to keep swimmers away, but Ray Grant's closing the trail suited him much better. He was delighted and couldn't wait to start building that fence, knowing that everyone but Beacon Lodge guests would be barred."

"So he must have been even more thrilled when Tasha flung the sea horse paperweight through Ray's window," Millie said thoughtfully. "Did you find out how she did it?"

"She didn't," I said simply. "Paul did. He knew about the fights she kept causing and was pretty sure *she'd* get the blame if he used Ed's sea horse to do the damage.

That meant Ray, who was itching for an excuse to keep out ALL riders, would refuse to let the Meadows family across his land any more, giving Paul and his brother more opportunity for their smuggling game."

"But the access to the cove is all straightened out too, isn't it?" Tom said as he looked at me. "Val and Ed were so grateful to you that they explained the whole thing, didn't they?"

I nodded. "All those important meetings Val's been attending were to investigate Ray's claim on the strip of land leading to the beach. Tasha was right – his 'proof' was a clever forgery and Val's been able to expose it."

"Phew," Tom whistled. "No wonder they didn't like Tasha's in-your-face methods. They were just going along with Ray's demands till they could prove him wrong legally."

"What, with a big court case and everything?" Millie asked, and she made a face. "That'll take forever, and I want to ride to the beach with Zak *now*!"

I laughed at her. "Don't worry, you selfish little cat. The fence is being demolished as we speak and Ray Grant won't be bothering Beacon Lodge at all in the future."

Tom let out a long whistle. "You don't mean he's going to jail?"

"No, Val didn't want to press charges about the forgery. She's just glad to be losing him as a neighbor. Ray Grant's greed made him totally unscrupulous, just as Tasha said. He swindled her uncle out of cash and this business with the borders was a blatant attempt to cheat again, this time to get more money for his house."

"He's selling?" Millie sounded surprised.

"Yeah, that's what it's all been about. He could have

asked far, far more for his house if he could claim it came with exclusive rights to a private beach. Mega money."

"OK, I'm following you so far," Tom said, frowning. "But how come he gave Beacon Lodge permission to ride across the bit of land he cheated to get?"

"To keep Val and Ed quiet until he'd done the deal with the new buyer. Grant thought if he told them he'd allow access for their vacationers they wouldn't give him any trouble, and at least it would give him time to complete the sale. He couldn't care less that as soon as the new owners moved in they'd probably want to exclude everyone from their 'private beach'. Tasha told Zak Beacon Lodge would soon be barred too, and she was right."

"Grant didn't know Val was working like mad to prove his claim was illegal," Tom said thoughtfully. "And presumably he also didn't know what those two brothers were up to out there on Tyber Cliffs. Paul should be locked up and the key thrown away for what he tried to do to you, Caitlin."

"He panicked. I don't think he ever intended to get *that* heavy," I said. "He's more of a small time, opportunist crook. I had a vague suspicion when I found the fence panel had been loosened. Paul was the most likely person to do that, wasn't he?"

"Hey, just a minute," Millie said suddenly. "It's all very well you becoming a Tasha fan because she was right all along and she helped rescue you, but what about that guilty look of hers you thought you spotted?"

"That's why she and Zak were in the cove. Tasha was confessing to him that although she hadn't smashed Ray's window she *had* flung the sea horse out of the window in sheer anger when she went looking for Val.

152

Zak's had suspicions about Paul before now and knew the guy could easily have seen the thing being hurled out. And that's exactly what happened. Paul saw Tasha go tearing into the house in a rage and was working right outside the window when she threw it. It only took him a few minutes to reach the Grant house, slip in through the panel he'd loosened and do the damage."

"You have to admit Caitlin's first attempt at being a detective has been pretty spectacular!" Tom tugged my hair gently. "I bet the Meadows family are ecstatic."

"They're pretty pleased," I admitted modestly. "I've got an open invitation to stay at Beacon Lodge any time I like."

"Lucky old you!" Millie moaned. "Swimming with Zak every day – how fantastic would that be!"

"Swimming with Jade is my thing," I said firmly. "And Jade is the real hero of the story. I still can't believe the way she came back to find me!"

This story was absolutely true, and every time I think about our adventure at Beacon Lodge I shiver with amazement at how incredible my pony had been. Life is looking better and better for the two of us. Mom got the job, and our move to somewhere beautiful along the coast is all lined up, so daily swimming could soon become a reality. It's going to take a while to get over my first ever crush – I still think Zak is gorgeous and I often daydream about the way he looked when he came to my rescue – but I'm glad he's happy with Tasha who, for all her fiery ways, loves every inch of him in return. I'm going to stay in touch with my friends Millie and Tom, too, and I expect there'll be lots of times when we talk about the extraordinary story of not one, but *three* sea horses.